The Roche Collection of

Traditional Irish Music.

Oak Publications
New York/London/Sydney

the roche collection

volumes 1~2~3

The publishers wish to extend their warmest thanks to the many institutions and individuals whose kind and generous assistance is greatly appreciated. Special thanks are due to:

Douglas Gunn
Michael O Suilleabhain
Mc Cullough Pigott Ltd, Dublin
Comhaltas Ceoltoiri Eireann for the cover photograph of Johnnie Mc Fadden and Jeannie Mc Allister of Lower Cozies, Dervock, Co. Antrim.

21 Iona Green, Cork, Ireland

Distributed in the United States of America, Canada, Central and South America by Oak Publications, a Division of Embassy Music Corporation, New York

This edition printed in the United States of America with permission by G. Schirmer, Inc.
8/83

Exclusive Distributor:
Music Sales Corporation
799 Broadway
New York, New York 10003

the roche collection - an introduction

Francis Roche began the task of assembling his collection of Irish music in or about 1891. The work culminated in the publication of a first edition of two volumes in 1912, and finally in a new revised and expanded edition in three volumes in 1927. It is this 1927 edition which Ossian Publications has now reissued with such care.

Roche wrote that he had produced his collection for "friends and pupils of mine, as well as many teachers and members of various branches of the Gaelic League". Its circulation proved much wider than he had anticipated and even though it never supplanted 'the book' *(O'Neill's Dance Music of Ireland)*, as the primary literate source for traditional musicians, there is little doubt that it had appreciable effects on tune circulation patterns and the popularisation of certain settings. Along with that, many tunes were rescued from the cruel but inevitable death-hammer of modernisation and now remain poised in print awaiting the moment of possible re-entry into the living tradition. It is a happy thing in contemporary Ireland that the decline in traditional music during Roche's lifetime was reversed, at least as far as the instrumental tradition was concerned, and that collections like this changed from being potential museum pieces to sparkling, gold mines of musical thought.

Airs, double jigs, reels, hornpipes, single jigs, hop jigs, set dances, flings, set-tunes, marches, schottisches, and even some of the waltzes once popular with traditional players in certain areas, are all presented in a careful and painstaking system of notation. His attempt at indicating sliding-ornaments is progressive for its time as an effort at stretching the limits of the notational system to cater for specific problems in the transcription of Irish traditional music. The attempt to indicate traditional bowing in Batt Scanlan's Chicago collection *The Violin Made Easy* and some efforts in the 19th century MSS of Canon James Goodman at capturing piping ornamentation are two other early moves in the same direction. In Roche's transcriptions of Airs especially, quintuplets blend with triplets and sextuplets in an impressive, if subjective, attempt at capturing some of the sweeping rythmic abandonment which is so essential to the passion within this music. But for all of that, Roche himself understood that the written note was secondary in importance to a first-hand experience of the music as sound when he wrote: "It is only from hearing by capable executants and from diligent study that these beauties and peculiarities of our old music can be fully appreciated". The new generation of readers of the present re-issue would do well to assimilate Roche's advice. Those who combine a low knowledge of traditional stylistic techniques with a skilled reading of musical notation should especially beware of substituting too quickly the written note for the aural one.

It is evident from Roche's writing, in particular the Preface to Volume 3, that he viewed his work as a necessary first step in some process which would only reach compietion with the appearance of a national composer, the Irishness of whose music would be beyond doubt. In fact, both Roche and O Braonain (in his foreword) display this particular bias even in the context of writings which show a deep grasp of the nature of traditional music and dance. We today have had the experience of seeing this music growing on its own terms, and whatever his original motivation in compiling it, Roche's collection with a new meaning in a new environment can only serve to strengthen and enrich this variety of Irish music wherever it is played.

Micheal O Suilleabhain

frank roche - a biographical note

Frank Roche as a young man.

(Photograph courtesy of Mrs. Margaret Earlie)

Frank Roche was born in Elton, Co. Limerick in 1866 and died in 1961 at the age of 95. The key to much of his approach to traditional music may be found in his father, John Roche, a dancing master of note and a classically orientated violinist. Ballroom dancing as well as Irish dancing formed John's repertoire and Frank, more so than his two brothers, Jim and John, was to inherit this facility with dance, holding at one stage the Munster belt for Irish dancing. Old John, however, from the beginning surrounded all his family with music and dance and for a time all three sons were sent each Saturday to Cork city, some sixty miles away, from nearby Knocklong train station for music lessons. Violin and piano were the instruments studied, and Frank selected the violin as his particular specialisation. About the turn of the century, the father and three sons decided to move into Limerick city to start a dancing and music academy in Charles Street (now known as Clontarf Place) and to live in No.3, The Crescent. The sons formed the music ensemble while John taught ballroom dancing to the elite of Limerick. Jim also was organist at the Redemptorist church in Limerick during this period and the academy was a great success until the father died around 1913 at the age of ninety. Contact with the home in Elton had always been maintained with the family travelling home every weekend by pony and trap for what was a three-hour journey. The academy began to go down and the sons moved out with Jim going to Tipperary town as church organist for a time. Knocktoran, the house in Elton, eventually became the base for extensive teaching of music and dancing by Frank and Jim who also travelled to such places as Kanturk and Herbertstown. In Millstreet, Frank formed a musical friendship with the local priest, Fr. Brennan who wrote the Foreword for his collection. The nationalist waves of the War of Independence and of the Gaelic League gave a new impetus to Frank's life and he determined to master Irish as a spoken language. In the late 1920's, he went to Kerry and stayed with a local native speaker, Mick Sullivan, who was to become one of his best friends. Certainly, we know that Frank collected some of his music material in Kerry but it is difficult to say just what proportion, in the absence of his manuscripts (most of which appear to have been destroyed). Some time later when land was being divided in the Elton area, he used his influence with the relevant powers in Dublin to ensure that sufficient land was made available for Mick Sullivan to persuade him to move from Kerry. It was Frank's hope that the presence of a native speaker in the area might contribute something to the language revival movement.

For the remainder of his life, he continued to contribute to the musical life of the country, by adjudicating at feiseanna, teaching, writing articles for the Limerick Leader newspaper where he criticised modern popular music and dance, and forming friendships with other collectors of Irish traditional music such as Mairead Ni Annagain, Seamus Clandillon and, in particular, Carl Hardebeck.

His last music publication was in 1931 entitled ***Airs and Fantasies - a book of operatic selections, ballads and traditional airs*** **Vol. 4.**

*** I am indebted to Mrs. Margaret Earlie of Ennis, Co. Clare, a niece of Frank Roche for much of the biographical detail presented here.**

FOREWORD.

Dr. Joyce has calculated that there are about 3,100 old Irish airs now in print, and that about another 1,000 remain unpublished in known MSS. He has pointed out also that there must be many other manuscript collections in the hands of private individuals throughout the country, while there exists a large number of old airs which have never been committed to manuscript. The experience of the present writer confirms Dr. Joyce's remarks. In the South of Ireland alone there are many districts which have never been tapped by the collector, and in which a rich store awaits some future Petrie. It is probable that about five thousand old airs are at present in existence—a wonderful monument to the musical genius of our ancestors.

This large collection points to a long period of great musical activity in the history of the Irish people. The airs now in existence, numerous though they are, must be but a fraction of those produced by our people in the past. When we consider the history of our country for many centuries—centuries during which musical cultivation was to a large extent impossible,—when we consider in addition that the airs which have come down to us, were committed to manuscript only in comparatively recent times, we are forced to the conclusion that the greater part of our musical inheritance has never reached us. The fact that so much has come to us intact, is a striking testimony to the musical tendencies of our race. Only an intensely musical people could without the aid of manuscript have preserved for so many centuries the large collection of airs we now possess, a collection such as no other existing nation can boast of.

It is possible to trace many of our old airs back to their authors, or to the period when they probably originated. Dr. Grattan Flood has gathered some interesting information on this point. It is to be hoped that he will incorporate it in a volume which would form a very useful companion to his valuable "History of Irish Music." But the history of the greater number of our old airs is lost to us for ever. Many of them bear evidences of a great antiquity. It is interesting to notice that poems are to be found in our early literature identical in metre with some existing Irish songs. To one who is aware of the close connection existing between air and metre in our Irish songs, this fact establishes at least a presumption that such airs, or some form of them, date back to the period of the olden poems.

Much of the character of old Irish melodies is derived from the scales on which they are founded. We may distinguish at least five such scales. They are constructed by taking each of the notes *do*, *re*, *mi*, *soh*, and *la* as tonics or fundamentals, and building on them a scale without the use of accidentals. Thus we have a tone, and not, as in modern music, a semi-tone at the top of four of these scales—the scales of *re*, *mi*, *soh*, and *la*. Errors in notation have frequently been made by collectors through ignorance of this fact. They have written the airs as if they were constructed on the modern major or minor scales, not understanding that Irish melodies have a scale system all their own. Another fact to be noted is that we have there minor scales in old Irish music—the scale of *re*, the scale of *mi*, and the scale of *la*. It must not be supposed that the airs constructed on those scales have always that plaintive character which we now-a-days associate with the minor scale. Many of our liveliest dance tunes are written in the minor modes.

In a large number of our old airs the notes *fa* and *ti* do not occur, or occur only as passing notes. Probably some of our oldest melodies are to be found in this class. The scales on which these melodies are constructed contain only five notes and the octave. They are known as the Gapped Scales. Whether the omission of the semi-tone be due to defect in early musical instruments, or to a defect in the ears of our ancestors, by reason of which they failed to recognise the semitone interval, would be difficult to decide now. It is not improbable that these gapped melodies had their origin in musical instruments on which the semi-tone could not be rendered, and that there existed side by side with them melodies which showed all the intervals, and which were rendered by the human voice.

The regular structure of our melodies deserves to be noted. Small as many of our melodies are, they are structurally perfect, exhibiting that symmetry and regularity which we look for in all classical forms. It will be interesting to the student of Irish music to examine the old airs and divide them into the strains of which they are composed. The intelligent student will in a short time be able to classify the airs according to the characteristics which they exhibit under this head.

A peculiarly Gaelic characteristic is the triple repetition of the tonic at the end of a melody. This occurs so frequently that it cannot fail to be noticed, but it is so characteristic that one must needs call attention to it.

It has been claimed that the Irish scales differ from modern scales not only in the distribution of the tones and semitones, but also in the very important matter of intonation; that is to say that the intervals between the notes in the Irish scales and in the modern scales are not identical, so that for example the Irish scale of *do* does not coincide with the natural scale of *do*, nor with the tempered scale as we have it on the piano. Dr. Henebry is the great champion of this claim. It is undoubtedly a fact that the intonation of the traditional Irish singer and the traditional Irish fiddler differs from the intonation of the modern singer and the modern violinist. It is a fact also that the old melodies lose much of their savour when rendered with any but the traditional intonation. Dr. Henebry who has the advantage of being able to play the violin in the traditional Irish style, is investigating this matter in a scientific manner, and we may expect much valuable information as a result of his inquiries. He has already issued a brochure on the subject, but as it appeared when he had little more than begun his investigations, it would not be fair to regard it as his final statement of the case. No investigation of this subject can be regarded as complete which does not include the method of tuning used by the Irish harpers. The harp was the most characteristic instrument of old Irish music. It was used not only as an independent instrument, but as an accompaniment to the voice. Might it be that there were two elements to be distinguished in early Irish music, the folk music which would be preserved for us by the traditional singer, and the music of the harper or professional musician, of whom no specimen survives? Any good traditional Singer or Violin-player can reproduce for us the tradition of the folk-music. It is only when listening to Owen Lloyd that we can form an idea of what the educated harpist must have been.

It is to be regretted, but it is inevitable that we should hear so much about traditional Irish music from those who are not competent to discuss it. On the one hand we have musicians who deny the element of traditional intonation. As they refuse to study the matter in the only way in which it can be studied, i.e. by listening to the best traditional singers and violin-players, their opinion can have no weight. On the other hand we have the extremists who regard every native speaker of Irish as a true exponent of traditional singing. Sometimes he is only an exponent of singing out of tune.

As far as music is concerned we in Ireland to-day are like the Queen in her counting house. We are counting all our money. But a time is at hand when we shall do more—when we shall begin to add to it. And just as the Queen's head may change on her coinage as the years and the decades pass, so we may look for change and development in our music, change and development that shall leave it none the less our own. The image may change on the coin, but the coin will be always the Queen's

The piano and the orchestra will have their say in the development of our music. These will render compositions for us in all the five traditional modes, or in such modifications of them as time may work necessary. But what of our intonation? Here we must be satisfied with the tempered scale as are all modern nations. But this need not prevent us from producing a school of music as essentially Irish as are the oldest of our melodies. France and Germany and Italy use the self-same scales, but the music of these countries differs as essentially as do the people. After all the great force which divides the art of one nation from the art of another is national character; so that the most essential element in the ancient melodies of Ireland is not the five modes, nor the gapped scales, nor the traditional intonation, but it is the soul and the spirit of the Gael which is revealed in them all. When Ireland is strong enough to reveal herself again in music as she has done in the past, that music will be essentially Irish even though it be built on the major and minor scales of modern times.

Still the old intonation may always be preserved in compositions for the voice or for violin solo. Whether this shall be or not, none can say. But it will be always impossible to give a perfect rendering of our old melodies except with the old intonation. Hence the experiments of Dr. Henebry have a special value; for they may preserve for future generations this element which might otherwise so easily perish. Then would our children receive the dry bones of our early music, but never again should they see it clothed in the flesh.

CATHAOIR O'BRAONAIN,
UM NODLAG, 1909.

PREFACE TO VOL. I

Although so much has been done for the revival, and preservation of our National Music of late years, as instanced by the re-issue of the Petrie Edition, the publication of O'Neill's voluminous Collection, Dr. Joyce's Collection, and other smaller collections as well, much remains still to be done before the patriotic work can be considered complete.

The present collection was begun about twenty years ago, and its production has been undertaken at the request of numerous friends and pupils of mine, as well as many teachers, and members of various branches of the Gaelic League, who wish to possess, something, so far, not obtainable, a handy, and at the same time comprehensive volume of reliable Irish music at a moderate price.

Being anxious at first to avoid cases of duplication, I thought to give only what, as far as I knew, had not hitherto been published, and to exclude pieces of doubtful national origin, but in order to produce the book required, I had perforce to alter my intention. Where however, such cases occur, it will be seen that the settings in this volume, as a rule, either differ from what have appeared in previous publications, or are better variants of them, and therefore, I hope that their inclusion will be excused.

It may be objected to by some that the work contains matter foreign to a collection of Irish music, such as Quadrilles, or "Sets," as they are popularly called, and other dance tunes also. That objection may be admitted as regards their origin, but they have become Irish by association, and so long as the people dance Sets, etc., it is better they should do so to the old tunes in which their parents delighted, rather than be left depending on those books from across the water containing the most hackneyed of Moore's Melodies mixed up with music hall trash, and, perhaps, a few faked jigs and reels thrown in by way of padding.

In preparing this Collection for publication, I have to acknowledge my indebtedness in the first place to Father Brennan for admirable essay, and to the following ladies and gentlemen for MSS. either lent or bestowed. Father Malachy O'Callaghen, Gormanstown; Surgeon Major Bourke, U.S. Army; Mrs. Jas. Hickey, Killonan; Messrs. Patk. Joyce, Glenisheen; John Martin, Kilfanane; Dan O'Leary, Knockaney; Ml. Mulvihill, Newcastle West; Patk. Barry N.T. Drumkeen; Joseph Hurley, Glenbrohane; P.C. Dwane, Pallasgreen, James Noonan, N.T. Garrydoolis, and Wm. Merrick, Tower Hill; all of Co. Limerick. Messrs. T. Bernard, Peter McMahon, Joseph Halpin, E. B. Duggan, James McMahon, and Martin Clancy—all of Limerick City.

Miss F. Donovan, Seafield, Tralee; Messrs. Michael Disette, Ventry, and P. Kirby Rathea, Co. Karry, An Paorach, Nenagh, Co. Tipperary, Miss Hannah Coughlan, Cork; Messrs. Jas. Sheehan, and Ml. Spillane, Castletown Bere, Co. Cork, Mr. Ml. Dwane, Four Mile Water, Co. Waterford; Messrs. M. Flanagan, Kilmainham, and P. J. Griffith, Rathmines, Dublin, and Dr. Annie Patterson, and Messrs. Boosey and Co., for permission to include the original Irish air by Dr. Patterson.

For tunes taken down from the playing of Messrs. Wm. Guerin, Knocktoran, Edmond Quinlan, Glenlara, and from the singing of John Walsh, Elton Co. Limerick; For airs and pipe marches recently composed by my brother John, and Gillabridghe O'Cathain, St. Munchin's College, and to my father for airs and dance tunes.

The existence of the "traditional style" is a fact now established, I presume, beyond question.

There is a peculiar feature of that style which I have endeavoured to introduce here, and to which I wish to direct attention. It is a curious "interval" or inflection, that was much used by the old fiddlers with striking, and often with charming effect (I now refer to the men *who Could play*.) In the absence of a suitable musical symbol with which to indicate it, as neither the appoggiatura, nor the acciaccatura would do (one finger only being employed), I have used an asterisk for the upward, and an arrow for the downward glide. These affect the notes over which they are placed.

The notes indicated with the * are stopped about a quarter tone flat, and the finger slid on to its true position. Those with the ↓ are stopped about a quarter tone sharp—except between F E, B A, and E D—and the finger slid back to its true position. In the excepted cases the glide is from the normal position.

The length of the glide, however, varies, but the ear of the experienced player enables him to regulate that quite easily. In quick passages, where the glide is not possible, the * indicates a quarter tone. These "glides" or "inflected intervals"—if I may use the term—are, as a rule, executed gently, and with great feeling, but occasionally some force is used according to the character of the music. They occur much more frequently than where inserted, but it has not been deemed advisable to mark them all. It is only from hearing by capable executants and from diligent study that these beauties and peculiarities of our old music can be fully appreciated. For those who are conversant with it, or for the pupil having a competent teacher, a fuller marking has been considered unnecessary.

Proinnsias de Róiste

LIMERICK.

November, 1911.

THE ROCHE COLLECTION OF TRADITIONAL IRISH MUSIC

Index. Vol I.

Airs.

Double Jigs.

DOUBLE JIGS – *continued.*

REELS.

AIRS.

éamonn an cnuiċ. (NED OF THE HILL.)

(1st SETTING)

*see Preface.

THE BOYNE WATER

OR PRAISES OF LIMERICK.

SUANTREE. LULLABY.

Cois leasa agus mé go h-uaigneaċ.

Bruaċ na Carraiġe Báine.
THE BRINK OF THE WHITE ROCKS.
(1st SETTING)
Moderato.
7.
Bruaċ na Carraiġe Báine.
Is truaġ gan oiḋre 'nar bḟarraḋ.
(2nd SETTING)
Andante con espress.
8.
An Sean Ḃoiṫrín Foiṫineaċ.
OR CAHIRCIVEEN.
THE OLD SHADY BOHEREEN.
Rather slow.
9.
An Droiġnean Donn.
THE BROWN THORN.
Moderato.
10.

Bruaċa na Suire.
(FROM JOYCE)
THE BANKS OF THE SUIR.
(1st SETTING)
Slow.
11.
THE BANKS OF THE SUIR.
(2nd SETTING)
Slow.
12.
THE MORNING OF LIFE.
O. Carolan.
Moderato.
13.
8va ad lib.

AILEEN MAVOURNEEN.
Alex D. Roche.
Slow.
14.
lower notes ad lib.
JIMMY MO MHILE STHOIR.
Moderately slow.
15.
DRUIM FIONN DUB ÓG.
THE YOUNG BLACK COW.
Rather slow.
16.

JACK O'DONOGHUE.
Spirited.
17.
D.C.
Dearbraṫairín ó mo ċroiḋe.
LITTLE BROTHER OF MY HEART.
Plaintively.
18
NORA O'NEILL.
Gaily.
19.
D.C.
Deoċ an doruis.
THE PARTING GLASS.
Moderately slow.
20.

"An Paisdín Fionn." THE LITTLE FAIR CHILD.

"An buaċaill caol dub." THE DARK SLENDER BOY.

"An Rós Geal Duḃ." THE BRIGHT BLACK ROSE.

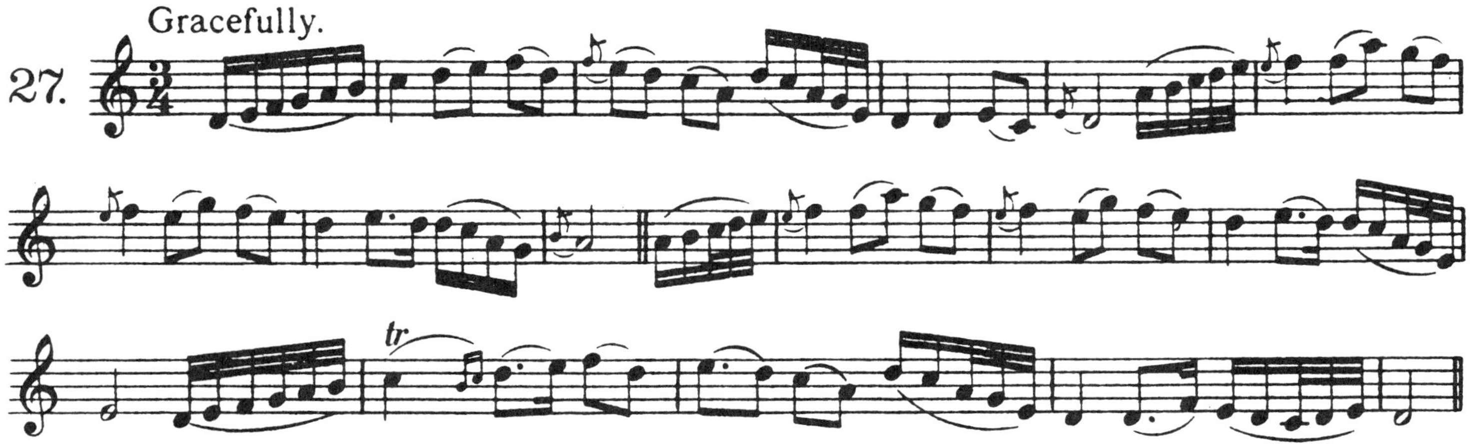
Gracefully.
27.
tr

Gráḋ mo Ċroiḋe. THE HARP THAT ONCE.

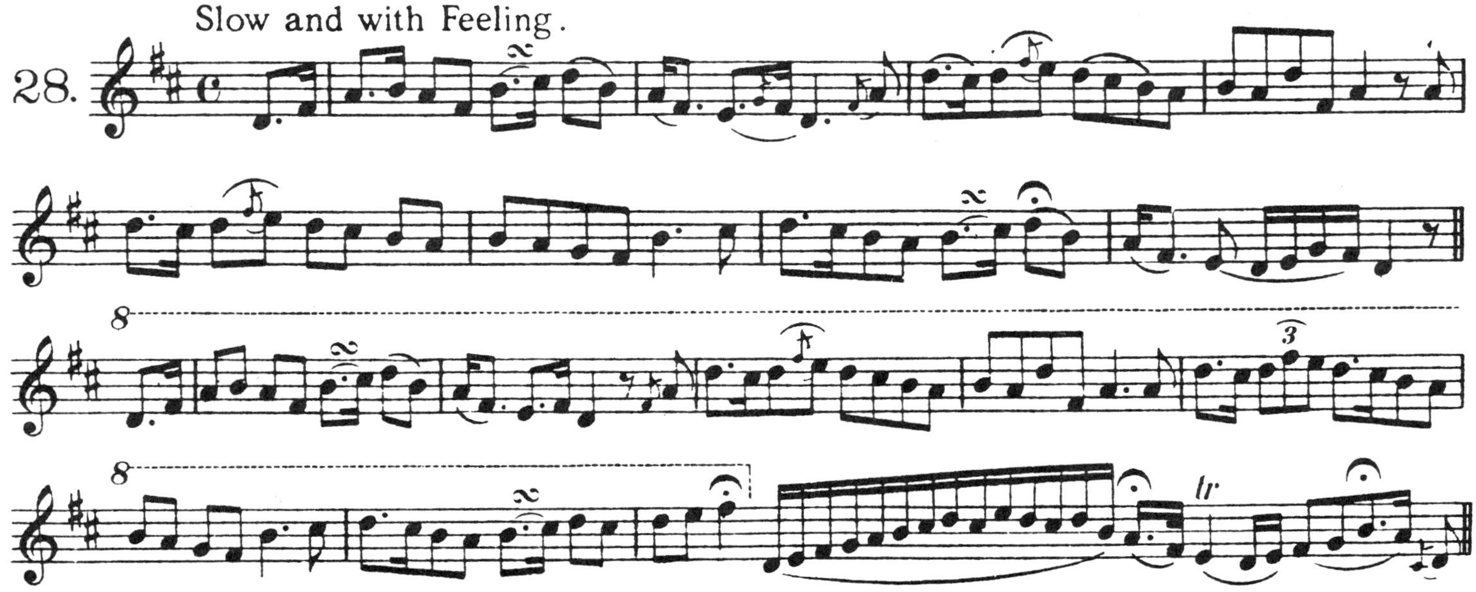
Slow and with Feeling.
28.
8
3
8
tr

"Siuḃal agraḋ." I WISH I WERE ON YONDER HILL.

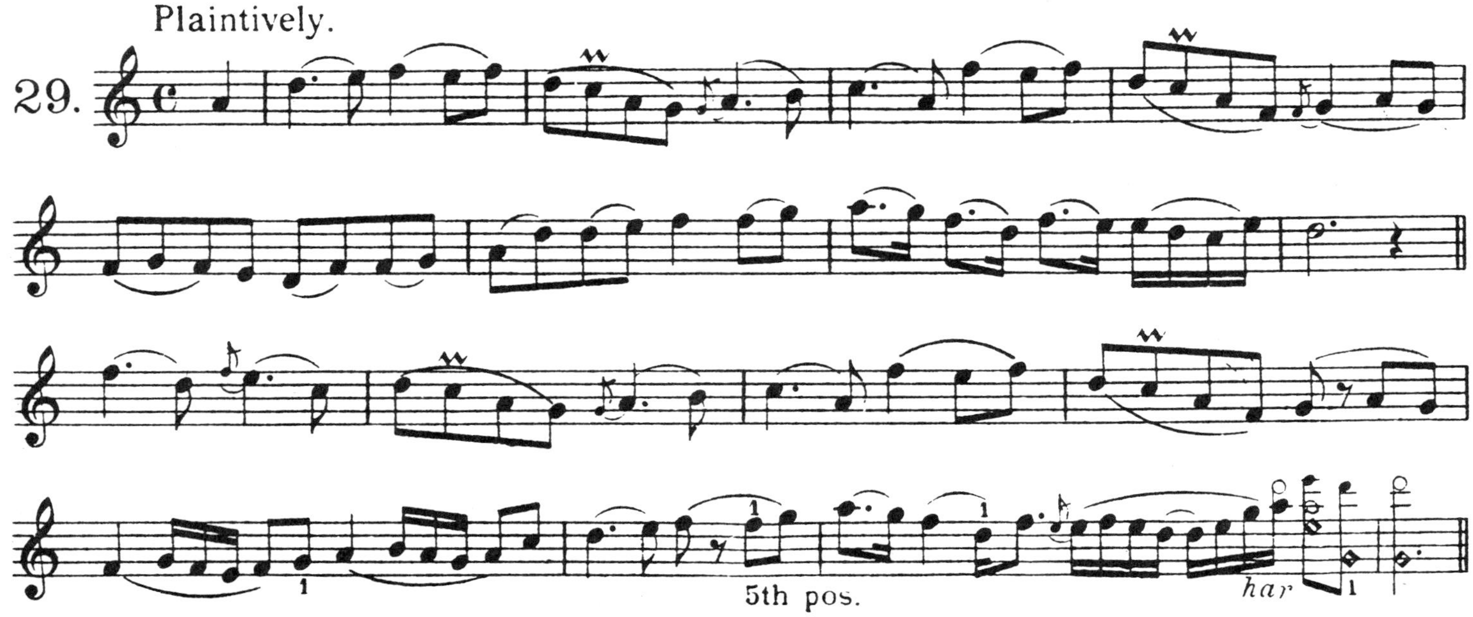
Plaintively.
29.
5th pos.
har

DERRY AIR.

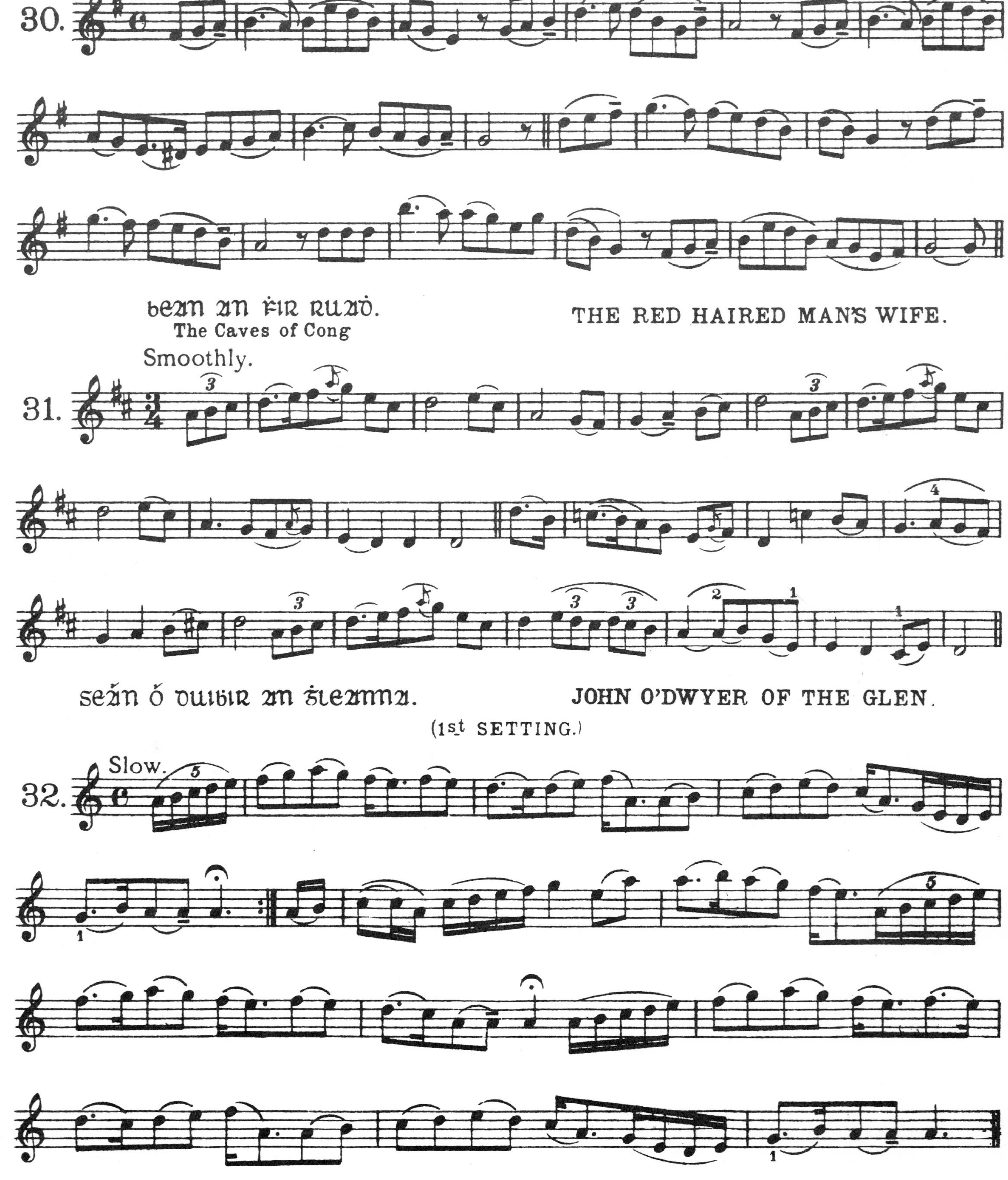
Slow.
30.
bean an ḟir ruaḋ.
The Caves of Cong
THE RED HAIRED MAN'S WIFE.
Smoothly.
31.
seán ó duibir an ġleanna.
JOHN O'DWYER OF THE GLEN.
(1st SETTING.)
Slow.
32.

Seán Ó Duibir an Ġleanna.

(2nd SETTING.)

Slow.
33.

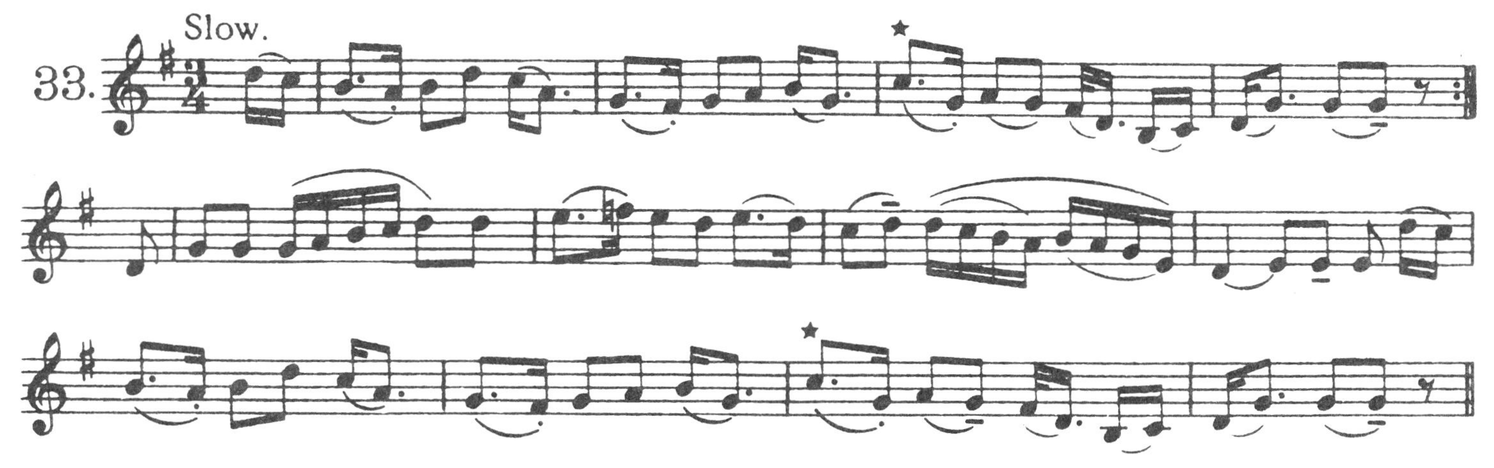

"THE GAME PLAYED IN ERIN GO BRAGH."

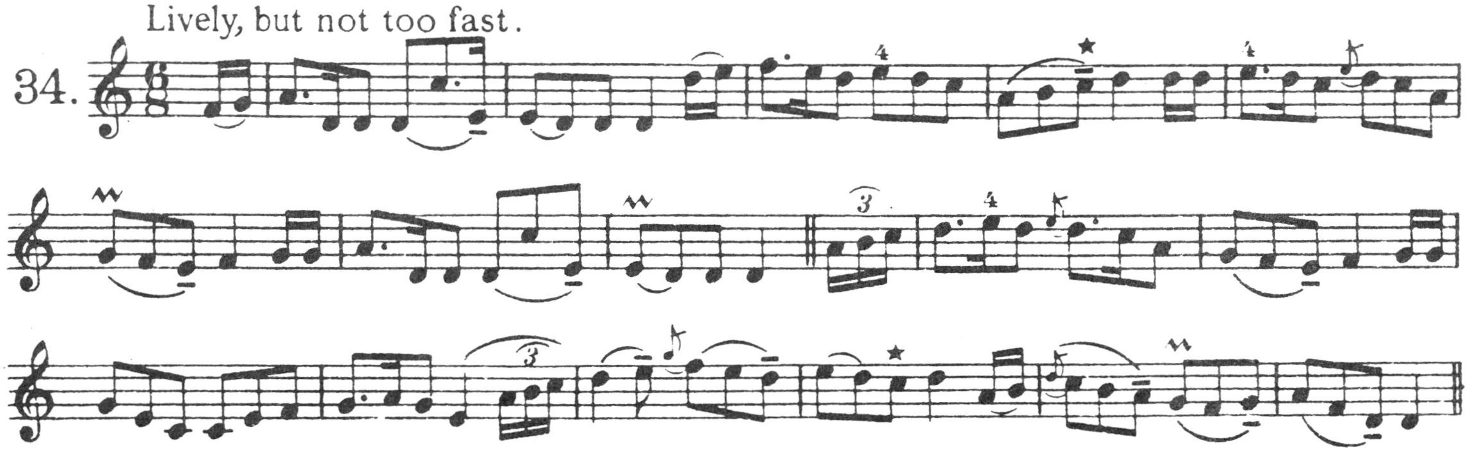
Lively, but not too fast.
34.

Turus go Tír na n-Óg. A TRIP TO THE LAND OF YOUTH.

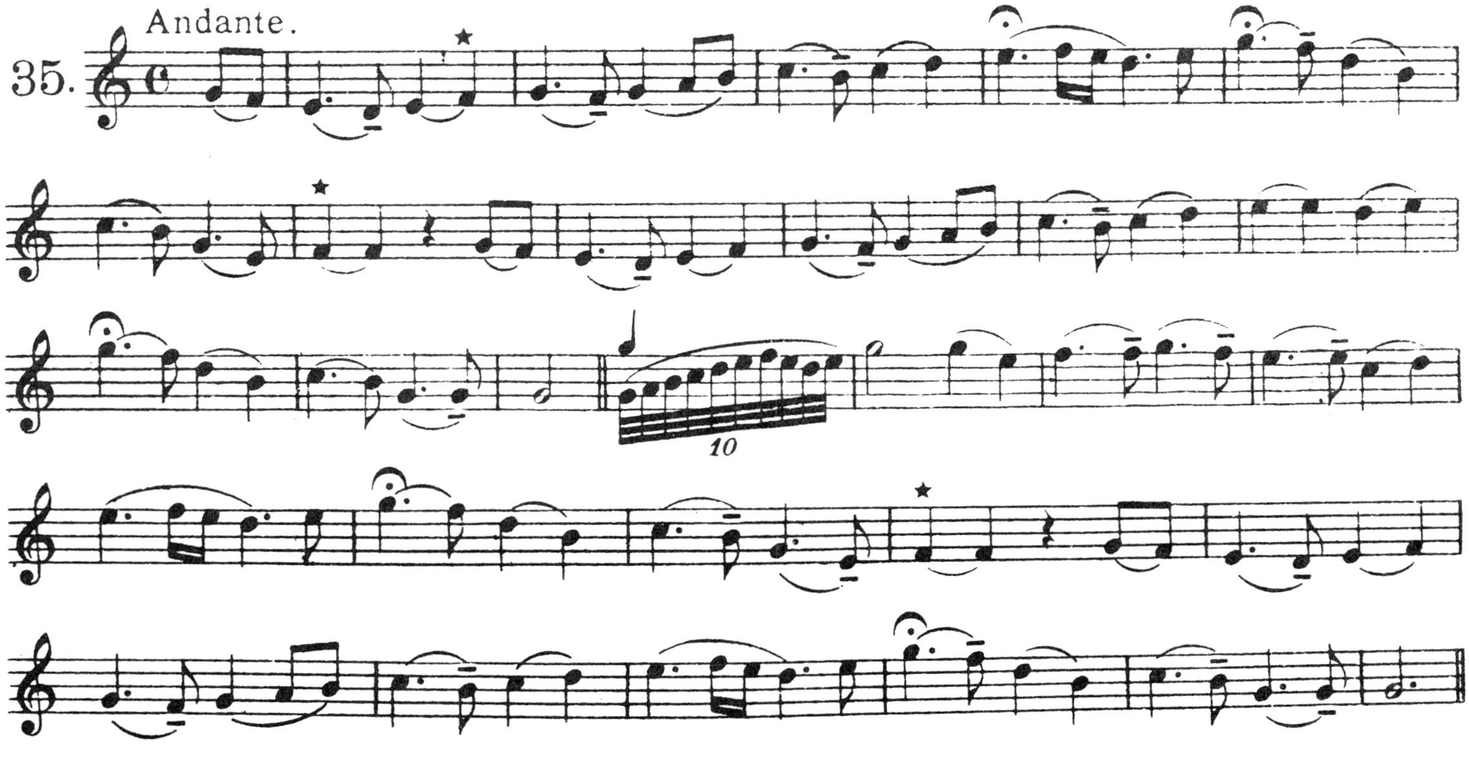
Andante.
35.

"THE HUMORS OF GLIN"

*ḃinn lisín aeraċ an ḃroġa
(THE MELODIOUS AIRY LITTLE FORT OF BRUFF)
1st SETTING

37

* For 2nd Setting see Vol. III p 17

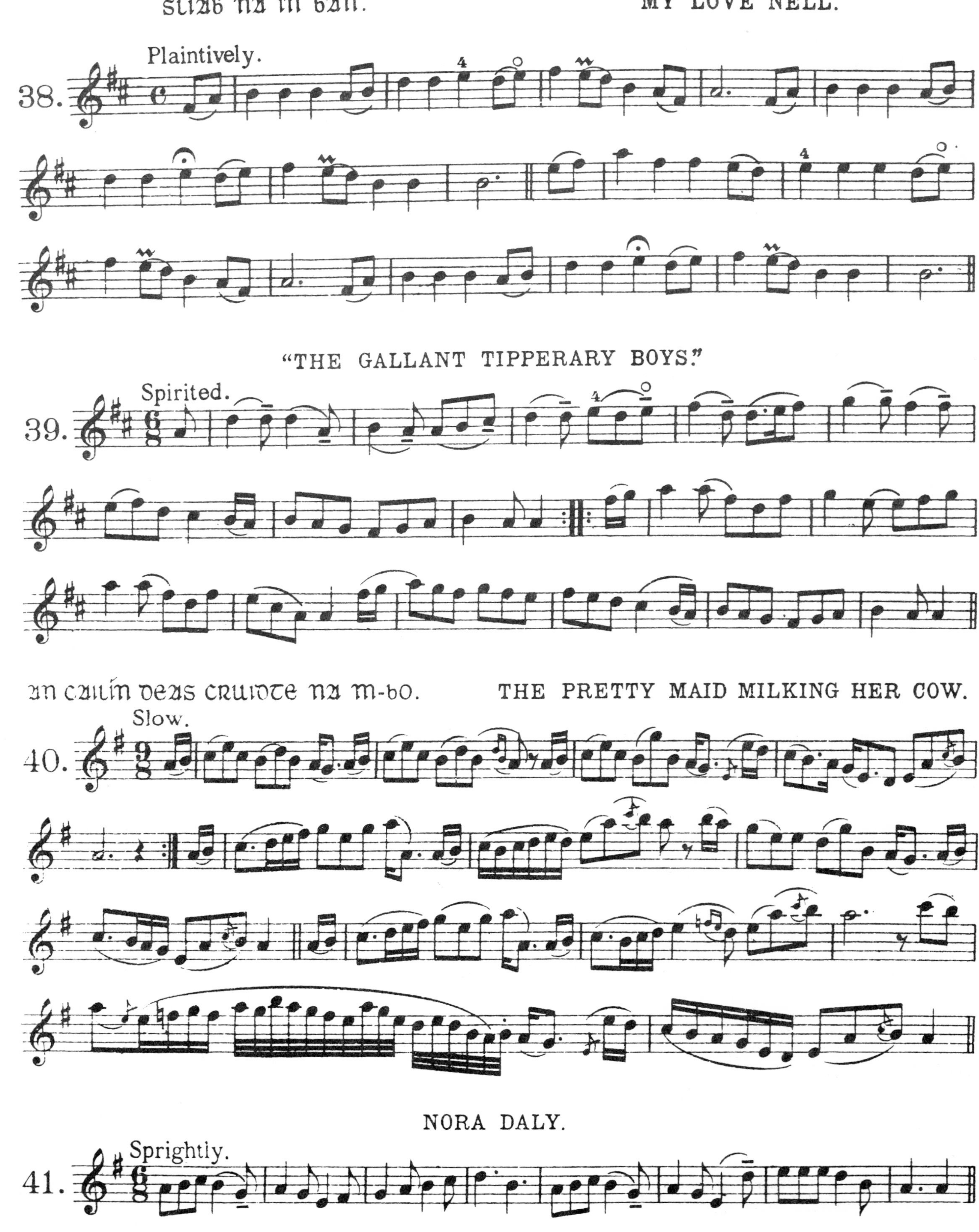
Sliaḃ na m ḃan.
MY LOVE NELL.
Plaintively.
38.
"THE GALLANT TIPPERARY BOYS."
Spirited.
39.
An cailín deas cruidte na m-bo.
THE PRETTY MAID MILKING HER COW.
Slow.
40.
NORA DALY.
Sprightly.
41.

THE GROVES OF BLARNEY.
(THE LAST ROSE OF SUMMER.)
Andantino.
42.
4th string
tr
pizz.
riten.
p
pp rall.

"THE COULIN."

An Cailín Deas Ruadh.
(1st SETTING)

THE PRETTY RED HAIRED GIRL.
(THE RED HAIRED MAN'S WIFE.)

sa ṁuirnín dílis. SAVOURNEEN DHEELISH.

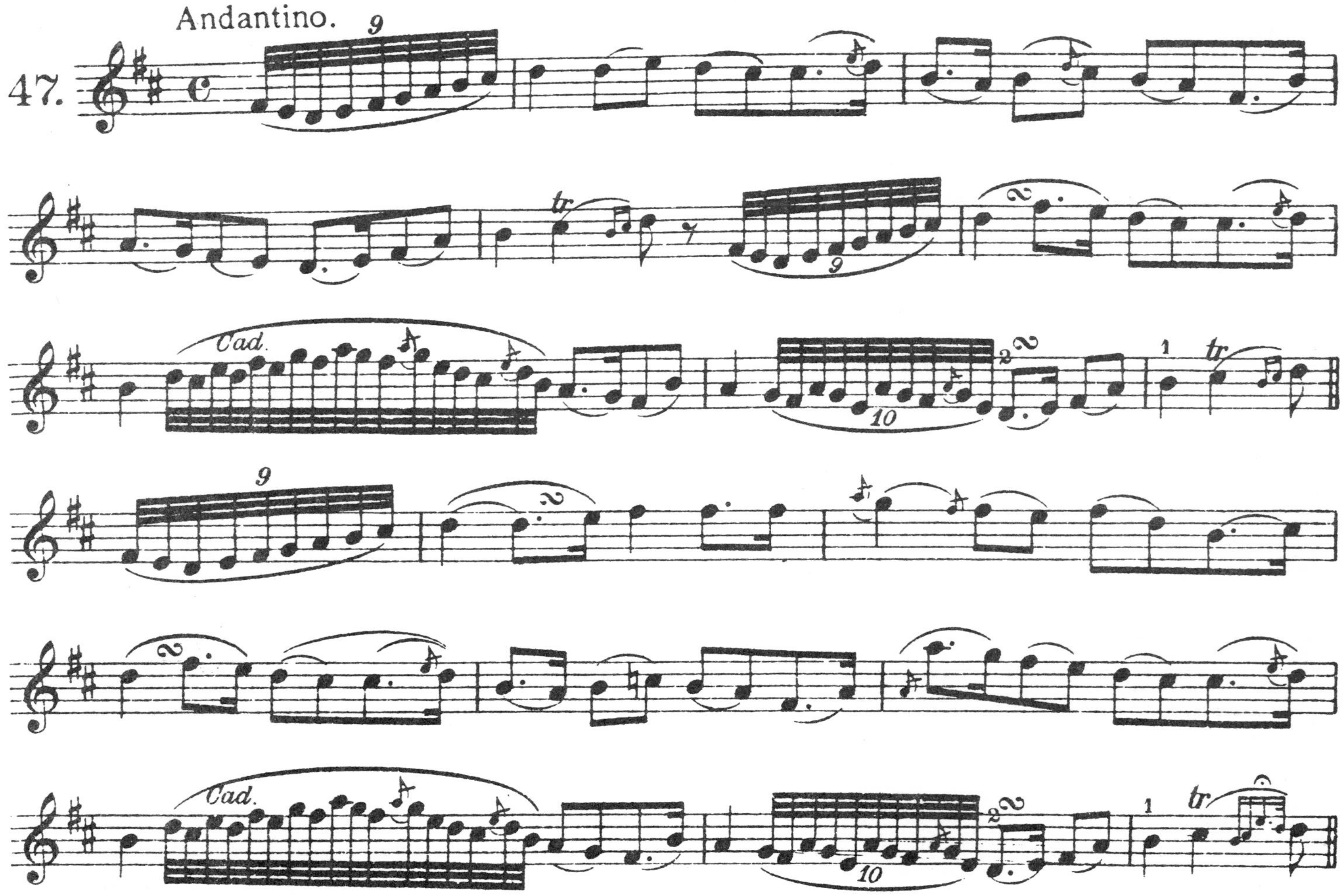

Andantino.
47.
Cad.
Cad.

*KITTY TYRRELL (1st SETTING)
O BLAME NOT THE BARD.

Andante.
48.

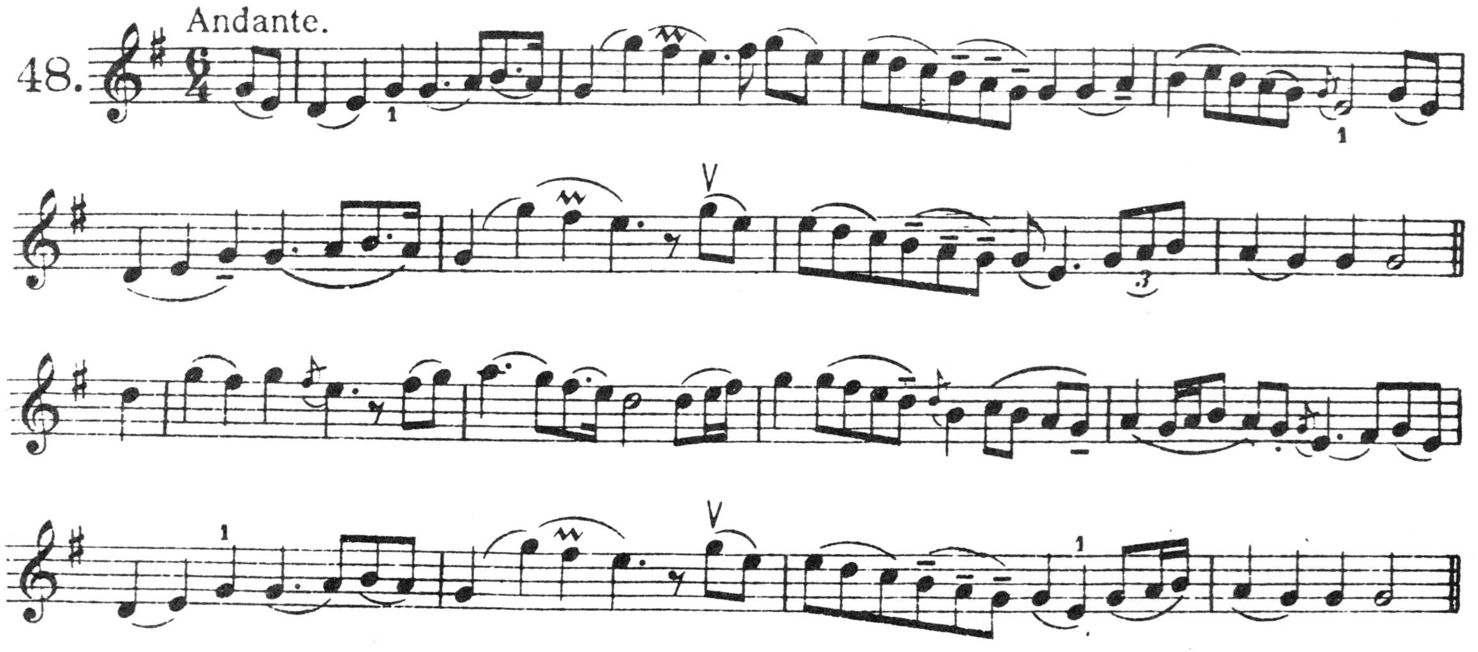

* For 2nd Setting see Vol. III p. 7

"THE DEAR IRISH BOY."

(1st SETTING)

Slow and with Feeling.

"REMEMBER THE GLORIES OF BRIAN THE BRAVE."
Rather slow, and stately.
51.
3
ad lib.
"MAURIADE NI CEALLAGH."
Slow.
52.

Táimse im' ċodlaḋ.
"I'M ASLEEP, AND DONT AWAKEN ME."
(From Moore's Melodies)
Not too Slow.
53.
tr
1.
2.
Táimse im' ċodlaḋ.
(Traditional)
Slow.
54.
"LOVELY SALLY."
Animated.
55.

"THE BLACKBIRD".

"THE DEATH OF STAKER WALLACE."
Slow and Solemn.
58.
rit.
rit.
a ċuisle mo ċroiḋe.
Moderato.
59.
DARBY O'DOWD.
Rather slow.
60.
1.
2.

An Raḃais aġ an ġ-Carraiġ.
"WERE YOU AT THE ROCK."
Slow and with Feeling.
61.
rall.
a tempo.
Ċáit Ní Ḋuiḃir.
Rather slow, and with expression.
Ballingeary.
62.
An Ċúiċín Binn.
"THE SWEET LITTLE CUCKOO."
Sprightly.
63.

"THE DARK WOMAN OF THE MOUNTAINS."

"LAMENT-FOR FATHER MICHAEL MOLONEY."
(Original Air)
John Roche
Slow and solemn. (con sordini)
67.
"COME BACK TO ERIN."
CLARIBEL.
Moderato
68.
tr

Seán Ó Duibir an Ġleanna.

With Vars.

Moderato.

69.

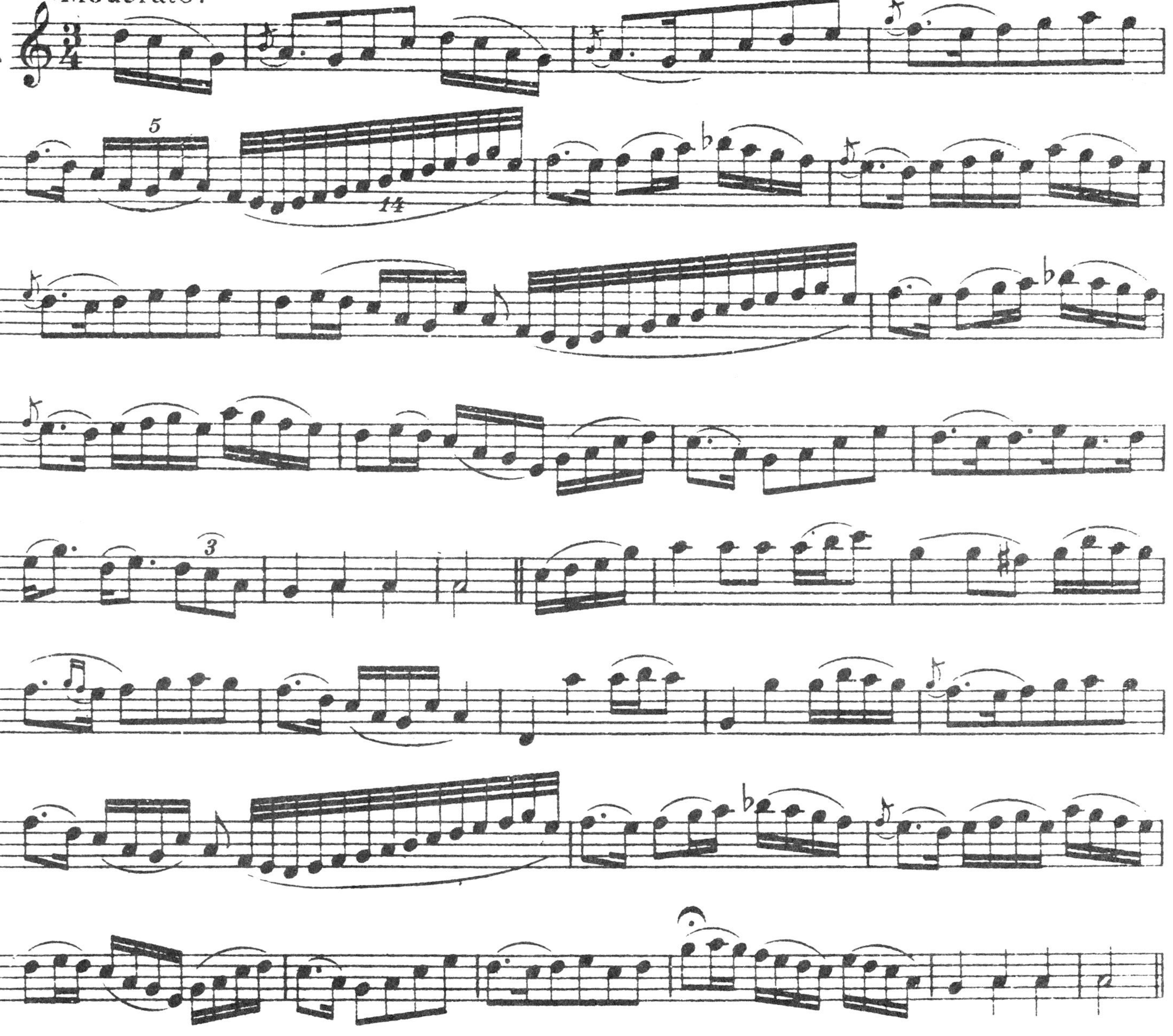

A ċailín big óig ná pós an sean duine liaṫ.

Allegretto.

70.

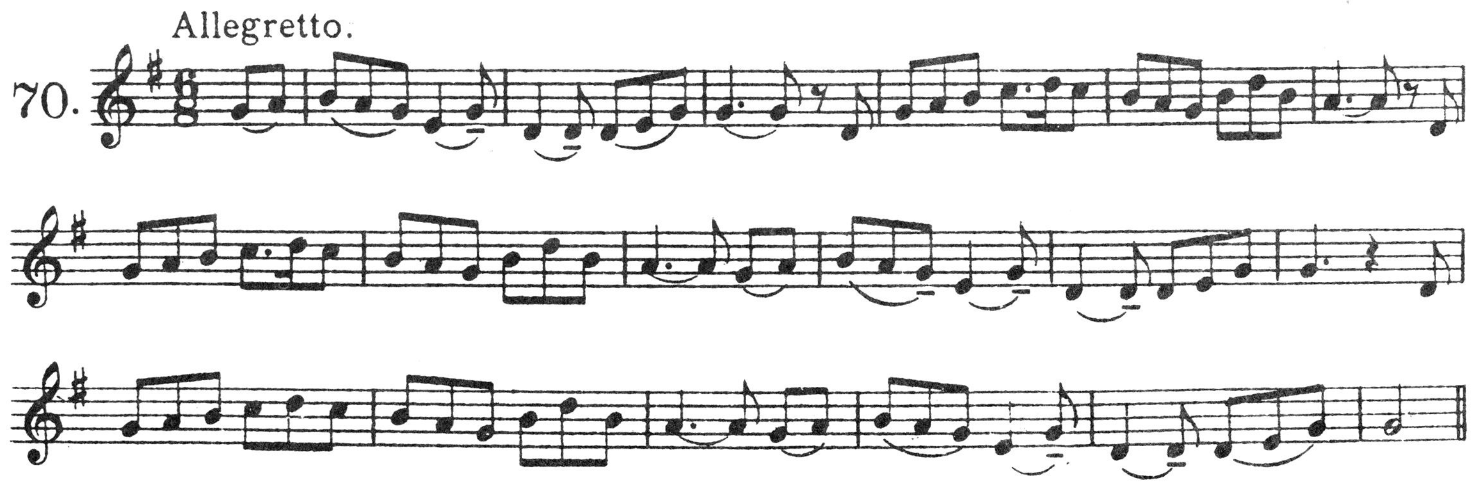

"KITTY MY DEAR."
Tenderly.
71.
4
4
An Tiġearna Ṁaġeo.
(LORD MAYO.)
Rather slow.
72.
3
MOLLY OGE.
Plaintively.
73.

"THE BOLD DESERTER."
Allegretto.
74.
"ERRIGAL M^c CREIGH."
Slow.
75.
5
"M^c LEAN'S LAMENTATION."
Moderato.
76.

"CONSIDINES GROVES."
Moderato.
77.
"THE OLD WOMAN LAMENTING HER PURSE."
Allegretto, With Feeling.
78.
"THE RIVER ROE."
or PATRICK SHEEHAN.
Moderato.
79.

DOUBLE JIGS.*

* The Double Jig is played for dancing with the accent – strong and medium – well marked. See "Note" on Dancing, Vol. III

"THE MAIDS OF GLENROE."
83.
"THE WHEELS OF THE WORLD,
OR THE DAY AFTER THE FAIR."
84.
"THE LITTLE BAG OF MEAL,"
OR "HUMORS OF MULLINAFAUNA."
85.
1.
2.

an buaċaillín buiḋe.
OR PADDY THE DANDY.
(THE BOUCHALEEN BUIDHE.)
86.
1.
2.
"THE GALBALLY FARMER,"
OR "THE RAKES OF KILDARE."
87.
"CHERISH THE LADIES."
88.

"THE WALLS OF LISCARROLL."
89.
"BRYAN O'LYNN,"
OR "THE HUMORS OF BALLINAFAD."
90.
"THE GEESE IN THE BOG."
(2nd Part)
91.
(1st Part)
D.C.
(3rd Part)
D.C.

"ROLAND'S RETURN."
92.
3
"THE SHOEMAKER'S FANCY."
93.
"GALLOPING O'HOGAN."
94.

"DONNYBROOK FAIR,"
OR "THE BOYS FROM THE LOUGH."

"THE GIRL OF THE HOUSE."

98.

"PADDY Mc FADDEN."

99.

"THE FRIEZE BREECHES."

100.

"THE KILLALOE BOAT."
101.
"THE LITTLE DRUMMERS."
102.
"STRAP THE RAZOR."
103.

"JACKSON'S MORNING BRUSH."

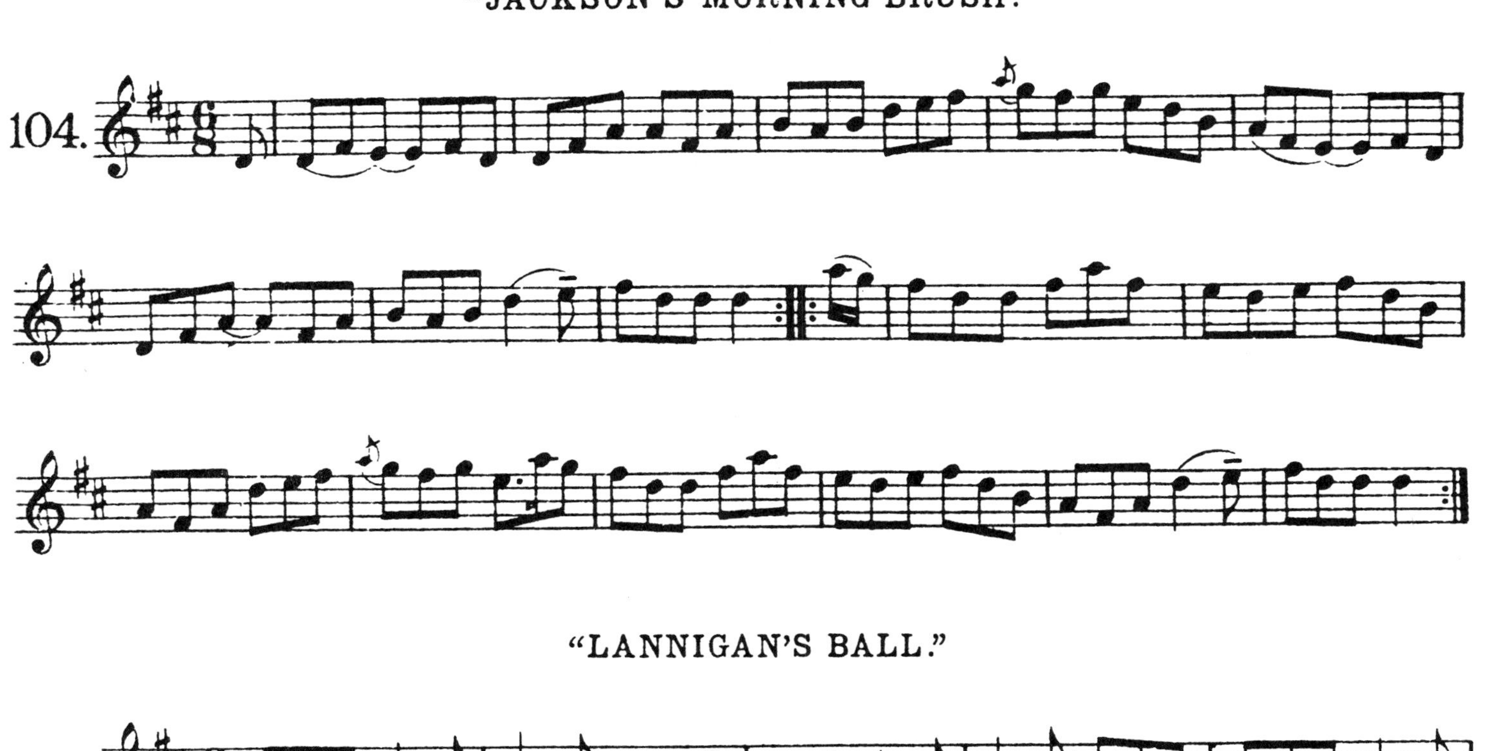

"LANNIGAN'S BALL."

"YOU'LL GO A HUNTING NO MORE."

"THE FROST IS ALL GONE."
107.
"THE MAID ON THE GREEN."
108.
"THE HUMORS OF CAPPA."
109.

"THE CONNAUGHT MAN'S RAMBLES."
110.
"LARRY GROGAN."
111.
"SADDLE THE PONY."
112.

"THE FLAXDRESSER."

balcais an blomaire. (PUT ON YOUR CLOTHES.)

"THE JOYS OF WEDLOCK."
119.
An buaċaillín bán.
(THE BOUCHALEEN BAWN.)
120.
"MOLLY BRALLAGHAN."
121.
"WHAT CALL HAVE YOU TO ME NED."
122.

An sean ḟonn dúr.
(THE FIRM OLD TUNE.)
123.
"THE PATTERN DAY."
124.
"THE EASTERN HARPER."
125.

"THE HAPPY MISTAKE."
126.
an sean fear cocailleac.
(THE COCKLED OLD MAN.)
★ 1st SETTING
127.
*See Vol III p. 28 for 2nd Setting
"THE CLARE JIG."
128.
"THE MAIDS OF TRAMORE."
129.

"THE HUMORS OF KILKENNY."

REELS.*

"THE MOUNTAIN LARK."

132.

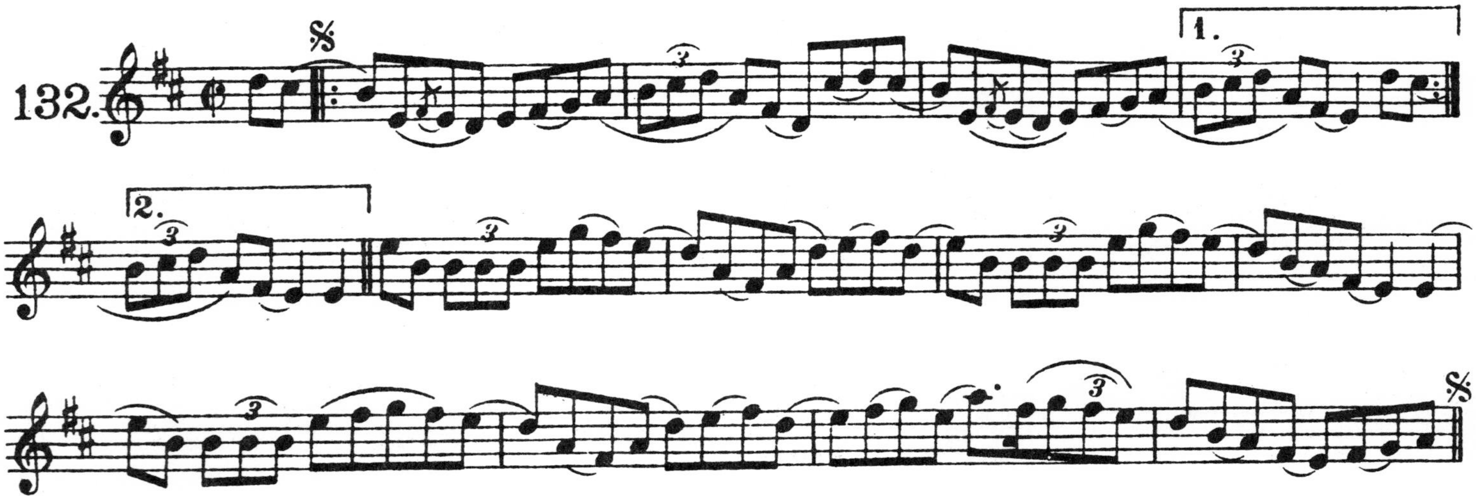

1.

2.

"RAKISH PADDY."

"SALAMANCA REEL."

* See prefatory note Vol. III

"THE GARDENER'S DAUGHTER"

"THE STAR OF MUNSTER."

Leabaiḋ Cailliġe. (THE HAGS GRAVE.)

137.

"TERESA HALPINS REEL."

"THE ROSE OF CASTLETOWN."

"THE MILLS ARE GRINDING."

"THE FLANNEL JACKET."

"THE MORNING STAR."

"THE HEATHER BREEZE."

"THE BUSH IN BLOOM"

"TAP THE BARREL"

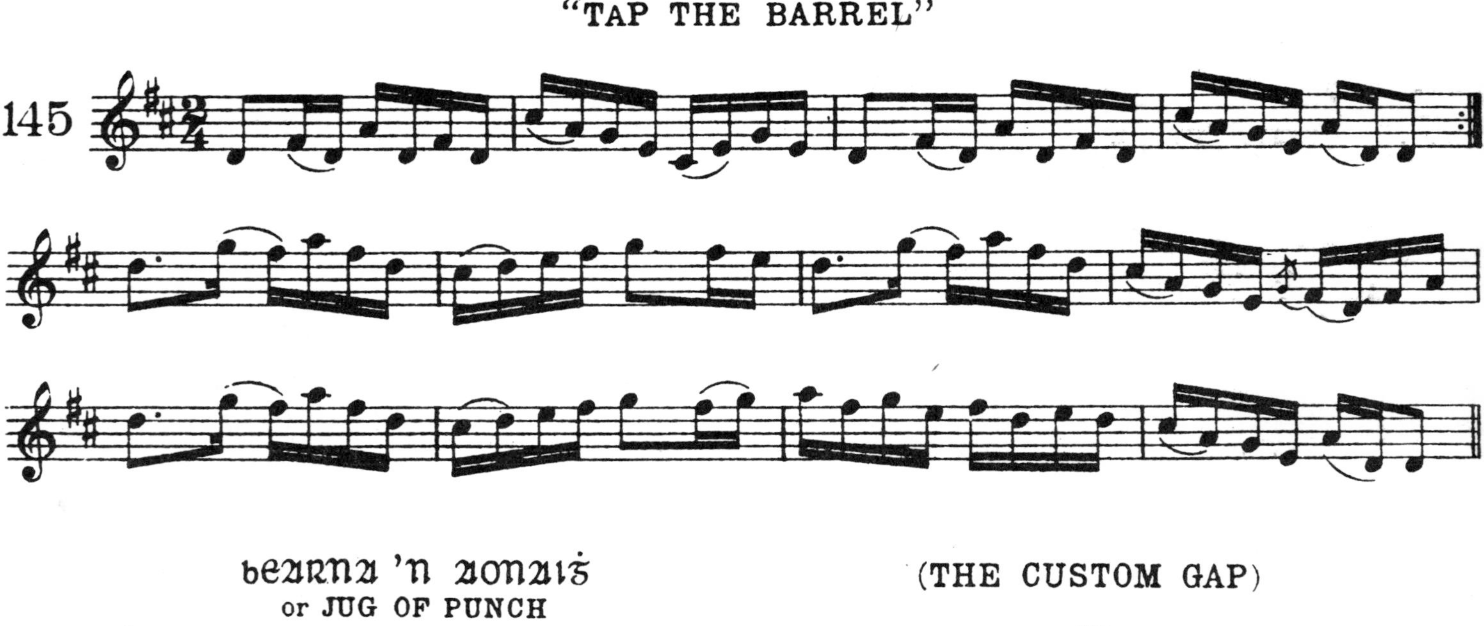

Bearna 'n Aonaiġ or JUG OF PUNCH (THE CUSTOM GAP)

"TOSS THE FEATHER."

"ROLLING ON THE RYEGRASS."

"CONNEMARA STOCKINGS."

"THE WILD FIRE CHASE."

*For 2nd Setting see Vol. III p. 21

"SPORTING MOLLY."
156.
"MOLLY BRALLAGHAN."
157.
"MISS MONAGHAN."
158.

"THE MAID AMONGST THE ROSES."

"MY LOVE IN AMERICA."

"THE OUTDOOR RELIEF."

"LORD GORDON'S REEL."

"DROUSY MAGGIE" or "PEGG IN THE SETTLE."

"MISS CAMPBELL."

"THE STRAWBERRY BLOSSOM."

"THE PRETTY MAIDS OF BULGADEN."

"MY LOVE AND I IN THE GARDEN."

"THE PIGEON ON THE GATE."
(1st SETTING.)

168.

"THE PIGEON ON THE GATE."
(2nd SETTING.)

169.

"THE SILVER TIP."

170.

"MISS LOONEY'S REEL."

"HOW THE MONEY GOES."

"MISS JOHNSON."

"TAKE HER OUT AND AIR HER."
174.
"SCOTCH SALLY."
175.
"THE MAGPIES' NEST."
176.
1.
2.
"THE PURTY GIRL."
177.
D. C.

"THE STILE OF BALLYLANDERS."

178.

"UP STAIRS IN A TENT."

179.

"JENNY PICKING COCKLES."*

180.

* All the F's in this tune are affected.- see Preface.

"THE CROOKED WAY TO DUBLIN." *
(1st SETTING)

* For 2nd Setting see Vol. III p. 23

"BONNIE KATE."
(1st SETTING.)

182.

1. 2.

1. 2.

"BONNIE KATE."
(2nd SETTING.)

183.

D. C.

"THE FLOWER OF THE FLOCK"
184
1.
2.
"THE BACK OF THE CHANGE"
185
1.
2.
"BUNKERS' HILL"
186

"THE LAUNE RANGERS."
187.
"THE DUBLIN PORTER."
188.
"THE FOUR MILE STONE."
(Set by Arthur Darley.)
189.
last time

"MARY OF THE GROVE."

190.

1. 2.

*Gleann Coise Binne. (THE MELODIOUS FOOT OF THE GLEN.)

(1st SETTING)

191.

1. 2.

* For 2nd Setting see Vol. III p. 23

"THE GREENWOOD LASSES."

"SPATTER THE DEW."
193.
"THE TURNPIKE GATE."
(1st SETTING.)
194.
"THE TURNPIKE GATE."
(2nd SETTING.)
195.

"POLLY PUT THE KETTLE ON."
196.
"STICK THE MINISTER."
197.
"THE KEEL ROW."
198.
"THE WIND THAT SHAKES THE BARLEY."
199.

THE ROCHE COLLECTION OF TRADITIONAL IRISH MUSIC

Index. Vol II.

HORNPIPES.

SINGLE JIGS.

HOP JIGS.

SET DANCES.

FLINGS.

LONG DANCES. (COUNTRY DANCES).

QUADRILLES.

OLD SET TUNES.

MARCHES. etc.

HORNPIPES.

"THE FIRST OF MAY."

"THE LITTLE STACK OF BARLEY."

"THE RIGHTS OF MAN."

"THE SHOWMAN'S FANCY."

203.

"THE FLOWERS OF ADRIGOLE."

204.

"WOODCOCK HILL."

205.

"THE SAILORS HORNPIPE."
206.
"THE CARAVAT AND SHANAVEST."
207.
"THE TAILOR'S TWIST."
208.

"THE LADIES HORNPIPE."

"STANDING ABBEY."

"THE MOUNTAIN RANGER."

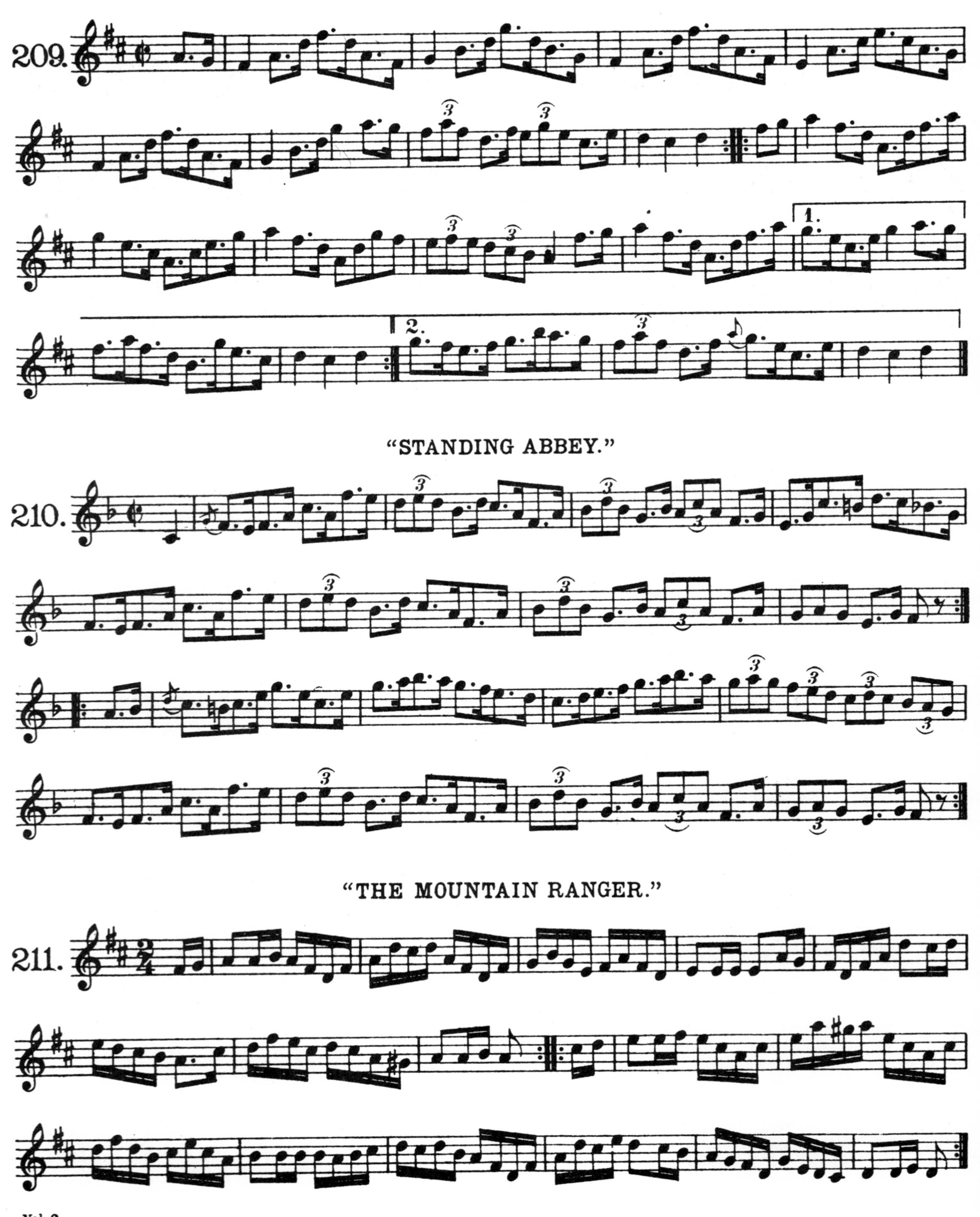

"BRIAN THE BRAVE," or "POLL HA'PENNY."

"THE PRIDE OF GLENNANAIR."
215.
"THE SOLDIER'S JOY."
216.
"WHISKEY IN THE JAR."
217.

"THE SALLEY PICKER."

"THE RISING OF THE SUN."
221.
1.
2.
an coṫuġaḋ muintre.
222.
"THE CORK HORNPIPE."
223.

"THE JOLLY TINKER."
224.
"THE PURE DROP."
225.
tr
"MISS LACEY'S HORNPIPE."
226.

"THE DASHING WHITE SERGEANT."
227.
An sean bean boċt.
(1st SETTING.)
"THE POOR OLD WOMAN."
228.
An sean bean boċt.
(2nd SETTING)
229.

Wings

March

Arr. for LHPE

Bonnie Charlie

March

Wayfaring Stranger

Religious Folk Ballad

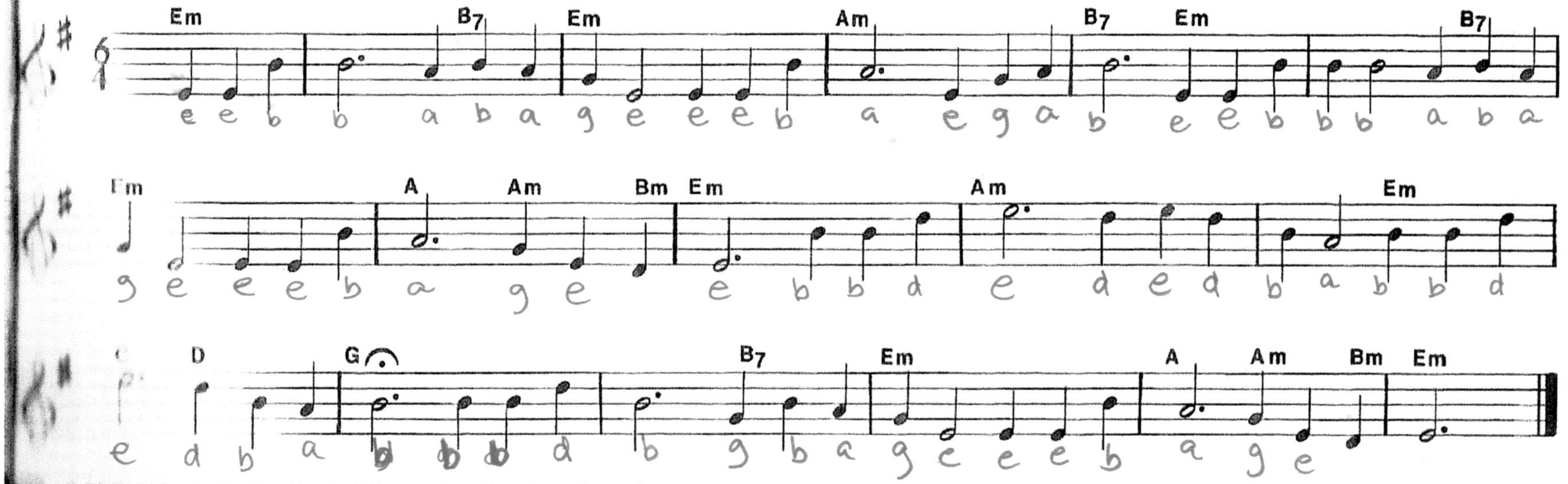

A FERMATA indicates the holding or lengthening of a note.

Scarborough Fair

English

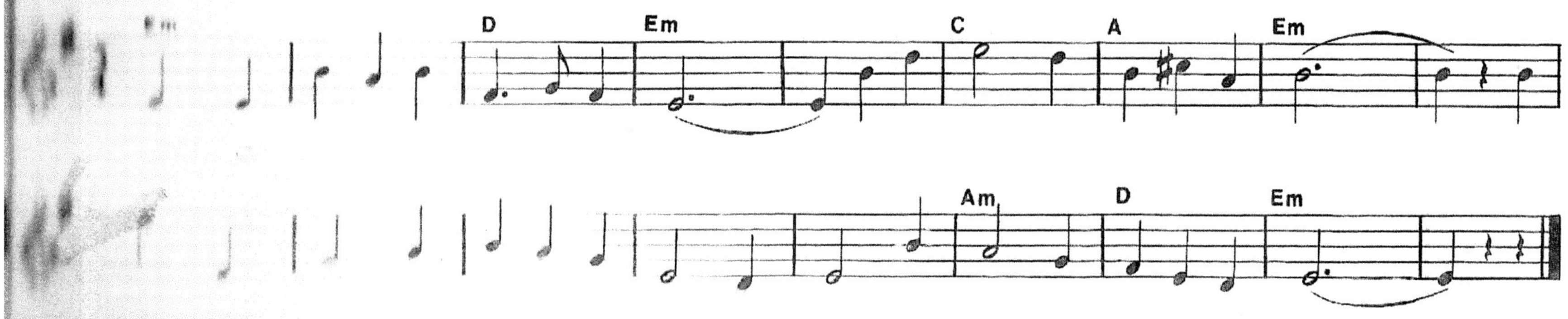

"OVER THE MOOR TO MAGGIE."

"THE FIRST OF JUNE."
233.
Faill na m ban.
"FILE NA MON."
234.
"THE GREENCASTLE HORNPIPE."
235.

"THE SPORTS OF LISTOWEL."
236.
"THE BLACK HORSE."
237.
An Spealadóir.
THE CUCKOO'S NEST.
("THE MOWER.")
238.

SINGLE JIGS.

"THE HEN AND ALL HER BROTH."

239.

1.

2.

"O THE BREECHES FULL OF STITCHES."

"THE PEELER AND THE GOAT."
241.
"COCK YOUR PISTOL CHARLEY."
(1st SETTING.)
242.
"COCK YOUR PISTOL CHARLEY."
(2nd SETTING.)
243.

"THE ECHOES OF KILLARNEY."

"RURAL FELICITY."
248.
1.
2.
"CAPTAIN JINKS."
249.
"BARRACK HILL."
250.
áṫa ḋúin an óir.
"THE GOLDEN PASS."
251.

"HOP JIGS."

"THE COCK AND THE HEN."

"HUMORS OF BALLYMANUS."

"BARNEY BRALLAGHAN."

259.

"THE BARONY JIG."

260.

"THE BERWICK JOCKEY."

261.

"UP IN THE GARRET I AM."

"A WHACK AT THE WHIGS."

"LOOPING."

"THE FOXHUNTERS' JIG."

"THE NEW WIDOW WELL MARRIED."
266.
1.
2.
"THE HIGH ROAD TO DUBLIN."
267.
"RUFFLE THE OLD HAG IN THE CORNER."
268.
"THE SWAGGERING JIG."
269.

SET DANCES.

"THE BLACKBIRD."

270.

"THE JOB OF JOURNEY WORK."

271.

"THE HUMORS OF BANDON."

272.

"THE SUISHEEN BAWN."

273.

"THE BLACKTHORN STICK."

274.

"THE GARDEN OF DAISIES."

275.

"THE HUNT."

276.

"THE JOCKEY AT THE FAIR."

277.

"RODNEY'S GLORY."

278.

An Fear Mór.

279.

"BONAPARTE'S RETREAT."

"KILLEKRANKIE."
or (PLANXTY DAVIS)

FLINGS.

"THE FLAX IN BLOOM."

284.

"JOHN ROCHE'S FAVOURITE."

285.

"LOVE WONT YOU MARRY ME."

286.

"KNOCKTORAN FAIR."
287.
3
3
3
3
3
"THE MONNYMUSK."
288.
3
"BONNIE SCOTLAND."
289.
1.
3
3

COUNTRY DANCES.

LONG DANCES.

"THE KERRY DANCE."
293.
"THE WALLS OF LIMERICK."
294.
3
"SIR ROGER."
295.

"OFF TO SKELLIGS!"

(QUADRILLE.)

3rd FIG.
TRIO.
D. C.
D. C.
4th FIG.
1st & 3rd
D. C.
2nd & 4th
D. C.

5th FIG.
1.
2.
1st & 3rd
(Repeat 8va higher)
D. C.
2nd & 4th
D. C.
"ORANGE AND GREEN."
(QUADRILLE.)
1st FIG.
297.
TRIO.
D. C.
D. C.

2nd FIG.
3rd FIG.
D. C.
TRIO.
4th FIG.
1st & 3rd

2nd & 4th
D.C.
5th FIG.
D. C.
6th FIG.
D.C.

"THE MIDNIGHT RIDE."

(QUADRILLE.)

4th FIG.
1st & 3rd
D. C.
2nd & 4th
D. C.
5th FIG.
D. C.

"OLD 'SET' TUNES."

302.
303.
304.

305.

306.

307.

308.

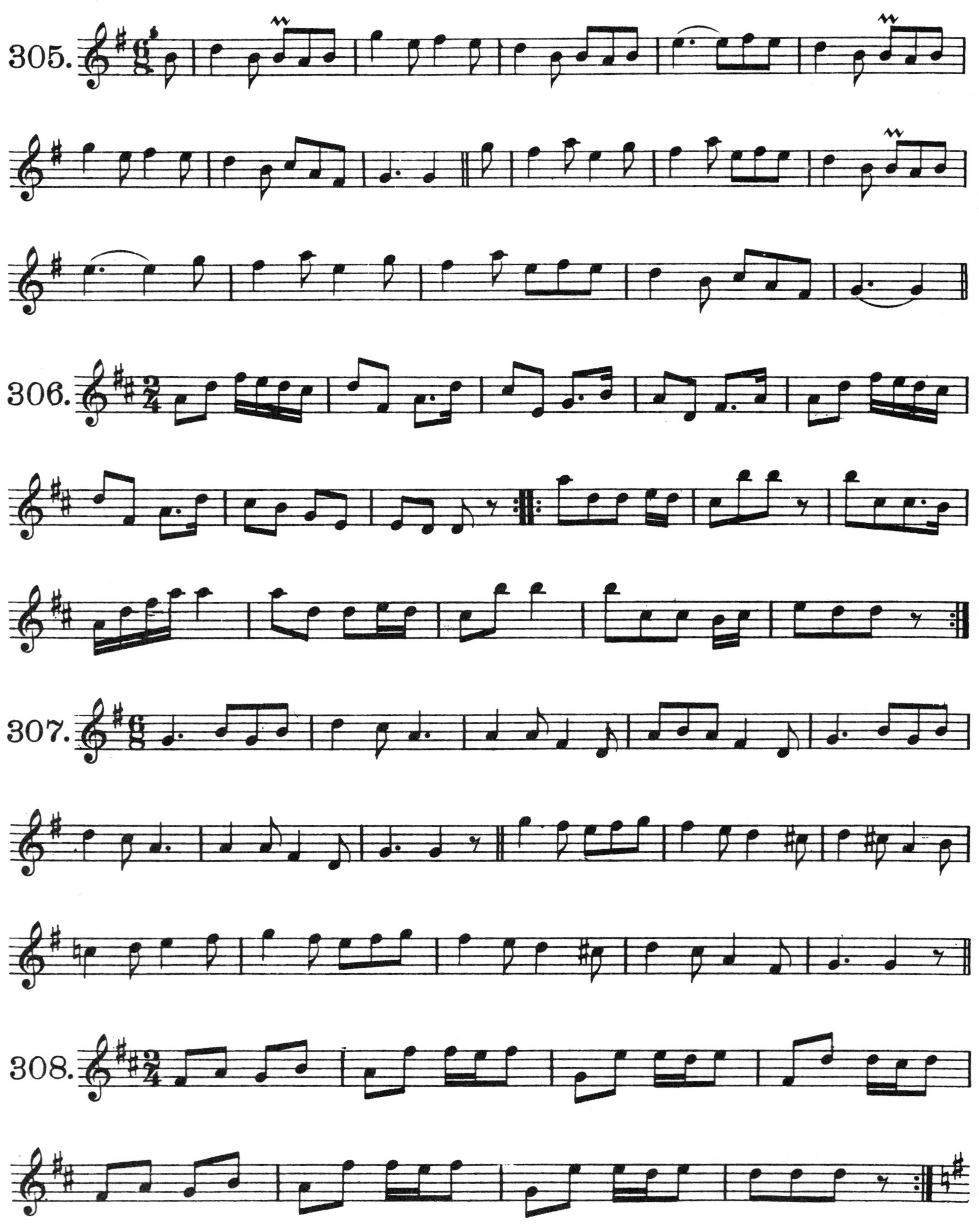

309.
310.
311.

312.
313.
314.

MARCHES etc.

"O'SULLIVAN MORE'S MARCH."

"THE FOLLING."

316.

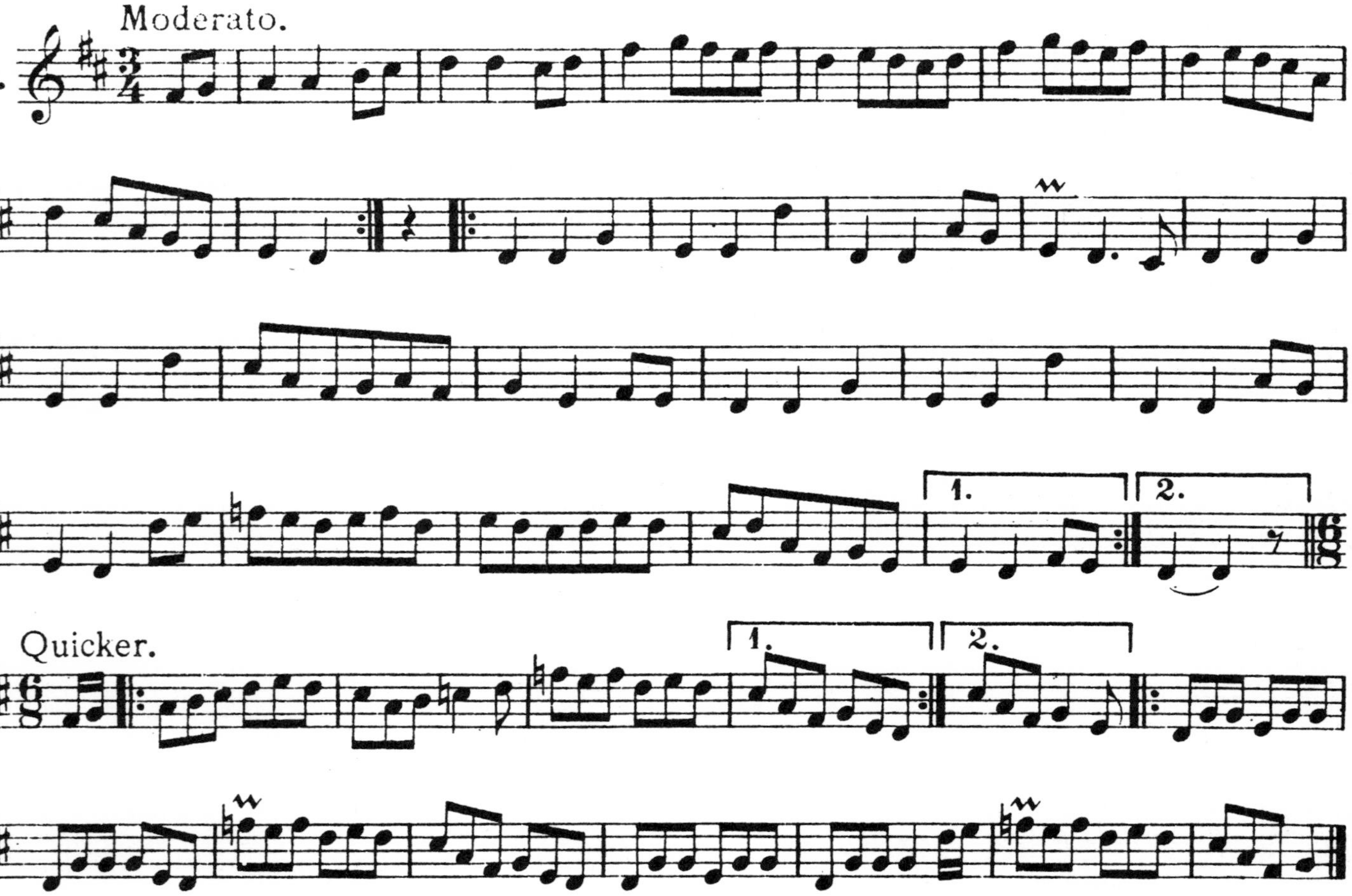
Moderato.
1.
2.
Quicker.
1.
2.

"CAROLAN'S RECEIPT."

317.

Spirited.

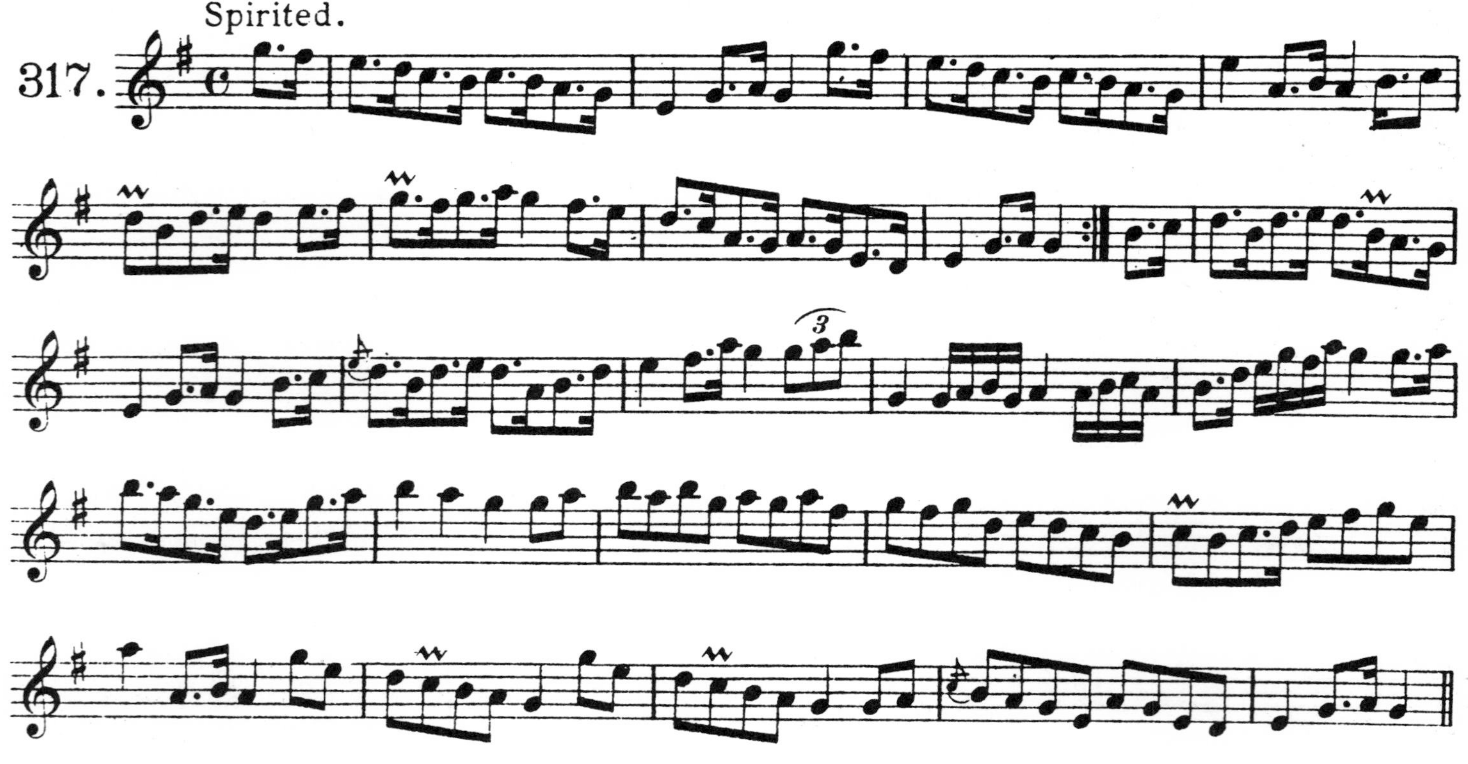

"THE CLOTHIERS MARCH" or Limericks' Lamentation.

"CAPTAIN BLUETT'S MARCH."

"O'DONOGHUE OF THE GLENS, WAR MARCH."
KERRY.
Bold.
320.
1.
2.
1.
2.
"O'DONOVAN'S MARCH."
HY FEDHGHEINTE.
WEST OF RIVER MAIG Co. LIMERICK.
Bold.
321.
"O'HEHIRS MARCH."
HY COROMAC.
CENTRAL CLARE.
Bold.
322.
"Mc NAMARA'S MARCH."
HY CAISIN.
EAST CLARE.
323.

FARRAH! FARRAH!

THOMOND OR DALCASSIAN TRIBE MARCH.

SLÁN AN ṖAORAIĠ LE LONNDAIN. (THE PAORACH'S FAREWELL TO LONDON.)

Ġiollaḃriġde O Caṫáin.

"THE SPIRIT OF IRELAND."

"ALLISTRUM'S MARCH."
(1st SETTING.)

"ALLISTRUM'S MARCH."
(2nd SETTING.)

"BRIAN BORU'S MARCH."

"ALL THE WAY TO BARNA."

YOU BROKE MY CUP AND SAUCER."

"PAT MURPHY THE PIPER."

MARCH.

"JOHN WITH THE LIGHT BROWN HAIR."

"KILLARNEY'S LAKES."

"THE OFFICER ON GUARD."

"FATHER HALPIN'S TOP COAT."

"RIDING ON A LOAD OF HAY."
Moderato.
343.
"KATE OF GARNEVILLA."
With Spirit.
344.
"BOB AND JOAN."
Lively.
345.
An buaċaill ó'n sliaḃ.
Spirited.
346.
"MARCHING TO DROGHEDA."
347.

"THE GREEN FLAG."
348.
1.
2.
1.
2.
"BAG PIPE TUNE."
349.
"FAREWELL TO WHISKEY."
350.
"SWEET CASTLETOWN BERE"
Lively.
351.

"GOD SAVE IRELAND."
352.
"MOLLY TIERNEY."
Spirited.
353.
"THE FOX CHASE."
With animation.
354.
1
2

An Madradim Ruaḋ.

Moderato.

stacc.

rit.

rall

FULL CRY.

accelerando molto.

rall.

a tempo.

rall.

a tempo.

rall.

a tempo.

poco rit.

a tempo.

rall.

p

THE CONFESSION.
Slow.
rall.
a tempo.
rit.
Caoine.
tr
rit.
Jig Spirited.

PREFACE TO VOL. III.

The first Edition (4,000) which appeared early in January, 1912, was so well received as to render a reprint of the work necessary after a few months, the entire issue having been sold out. Two further reprints have since been called for.

This affords gratifying evidence that the labour of collecting, arranging and editing, has not been unappreciated by the Music-loving people of Ireland.

Encouraged by that success, and in response to numerous requests, the enterprising publishers had decided some years ago on bringing out another edition of the whole Collection, arranged for the Pianoforte by Dr. Annie Patterson—of whose eminence as a Musician, and enthusiasm in the cause of Irish Music, it is unnecessary to speak—but its publication has been unavoidably delayed by circumstances arising out of the great war.

In harmonizing these Airs, it has been the aim of Dr. Patterson to make them—in her own words—" as Musically acceptable as possible " (keeping in view, doubtless, subsequent instrumental and Orchestral arrangements), and to endeavour to demonstrate their adaptability to as full a harmonization as the Folk Music of other Nations. That she has succeeded in her object will, I am sure, be generally conceded, particularly in her treatment of those pieces in the Modal Major, and Diatonic Scales, but with regard to the Ancient Minors—a delicate question—a diversity of opinion may be expected.

The compilation involved considerable labour, but it was a labour of love lightened always by the consciousness of its national import and necessity. Looking at it now fully harmonized, I cannot help reflecting how, in boyhood, when listening with delight to many of these fine old Airs and pieces—notably " The Fox Chase "—I used at the same time, feel sad to think that they could never, as it then seemed, be noted down, but would pass away with the old patriots who played them. I little thought at the time that the day was not so far off, when not alone would they be noted down, but harmonized, and that the performance of the famous old " Fox Chase " by a full Orchestra would also be made possible. Ni Misde a radh go deimhin, agus gan a bheith a' maoidheamh as, go bhfuil céim mor buailte ar aighidh againn o shoin.

If playing from the Pianoforte arrangement, the Violinist should observe that the Melody has always the tails up except where the harmony is mostly in the bass. When accompanying the Violin the Pianist should leave the Melody to the latter, and fill in from the harmony provided, but in loud passages, for special effects, or in playing for Dancing this need not be adhered to. A separate Violin part is issued for those who play only the Violin, Flute or Pipes, or for any who may object to Pianoforte arrangements on traditional grounds. This separate part is necessary also in order to preserve the historical significance, and continuity of our Old Music, as Dr. Annie Patterson, owing probably to the exigencies of harmony, has in a few cases altered the key signatures, and in many others supplied endings that might, possibly, mislead the student as to their antiquity.*

The Collection has been completely revised and enlarged by more than 200 Airs and various pieces taken down and collected during the past few years, amongst them some fine settings of Airs from an old MS. of my father's which was not available when the first edition was being prepared. These were all embodied in Vols. I and II, according to classification, and in keeping with the original design, and their production in this form was contemplated for a New Edition in three Volumes, but financial and other considerations precluded the idea, and necessitated their publication in a separate volume. I have gratefully to acknowledge my thanks for the loan of an old MS. book belonging to the late Mr. P. O'Donohue, Ballyneety, Limerick, and in particular to Mr. P. J. Joyce (now deceased), Glenisheen, Kilmallock, for many beautiful Airs and Dance Tunes, and for the loan of his fine MS. Collection of Irish Music ; to my brother John, and to Mr. Tim Crowe, Dundrum, Co. Tipperary, for some Airs and dance tunes, and to any whose names may have been inadvertently omitted. In compliance with the wishes of many, and in accordance with my own, I have included a selection of old ballroom dance favourites in this volume. In these simple and melodious items, together with the various sets of quadrilles, or lancers, a substitute may be found to some extent for the vulgar, inane, and noisy stuff called dance music in vogue at present. Let us hope that they may also help in some measure to enkindle a desire for a revival of the rational and artistic style of dancing which obtained before the war.

* The publication of the Pianoforte arrangement seemed assured at the time the foregoing was written.

PREFACE TO VOL. III—*continued.*

Some features of the " traditional style " have been referred to in the earlier preface. Other features of it are the compromised semitones between Mi and Fa, Ti and Do, together with the intricate syncopated bowings and the various graces and embellishments. A high pitch or rough robust tone, particularly in the old airs, is not in consonance with the traditional style on the Violin.

Care has been taken to avoid all errors in notation, to set the various pieces in their true scales, and to fully indicate the bowing ; to preserve the old " blas," and to present them in such a manner that, when properly performed, all their peculiar merits and characteristics may be truly estimated.

The completion of this volume brings to a close my work as a collector of Irish Airs. There now remains but little to accomplish in this domain if we may judge by the small number of hitherto unpublished airs that have appeared in recent years, and by the many instances of duplication to be found in the various collections—my own included. A few stray gems, however, may still be discovered to reward the diligent searcher.

Our policy and ambition for the future should be to make full use of the great store already in our possession, and to found and equip a truly national School of Music which may yet give us a Chopin, a Grieg, a Sarasate, a Weber or a Wieniawski to bring to fruition the seed that has been garnered by the devotion of the collector.

It is my earnest hope that the present Collection may serve somewhat towards the realisation of this great ideal.

Proinsias de Roiste.

Cnoctorann, Cnocluinge, Co. Luimnighe.

Samhain, 1927.

NOTE ON IRISH DANCING.

A few remarks on certain aspects of Irish Dancing, as they affect our National Music, may form a suitable introduction to a Collection in which our dance tunes are such a prominent feature.

Up to the beginning of the present century, or for some time thereafter, the traditional style of dancing the Jig, Reel, Hornpipe and many social figure dances—four and eight-hand jigs and reels, etc.—was in vogue amongst a considerable number of our people, and was still taught by a few of the old masters of the art, but as these retired or passed away a notable and regrettable change set in ; the old style began to wane until, as time wore on, it became submerged in what has been called " revival dancing," with injurious effects on our dance music.

This deterioration did not materially affect the double Jig tunes as these continued to be extensively played, the dance itself having been kept up with vigour, but the style peculiar to this, and the hornpipe for females no longer survived, and it was not unusual to find numbers of both sexes competing in the same items, and dancing the same kind of steps at Feiseanna and Aeridheachta.

It was unfortunate that in the general scheme to recreate an Irish Ireland the work of preserving or reviving our old national dances should have largely fallen to the lot of those who were but poorly equipped for the task. For the most part they were lacking in insight, and a due appreciation of the pure old style, and had, as it appears, but a slender knowledge of the old repertoire.

For instance, the Single and Hop Jigs, the Fling—*Irish version*—the fine solid Double Reel for men, and the sprightly Single Hornpipe for females, as well as many of our Set Dances must, if known to them, have been regarded as possessing neither Artistic, Social nor National value, as they all either languished or died out during the period of their activities, the result being that some of the best and most characteristic of our dance tunes were never heard at all.

The musicians were, apparently, as slack in tunes as most of the others proved to have been in dances. Despite the great extent and variety of our dance music a few only of the more commonplace single reels and double hornpipes were to be heard during the years under discussion. The Double Reel and Single Hornpipe were never touched, but those few were specialised in ; they were served out on all occasions with unfailing regularity, and an assurance not always commendable, until, through constant and excessive hacking, they had become a downright infliction. But the musicians were not entirely to blame, for the dancers, having in most cases been taught certain dances to one particular tune only, could keep time to no other—the single and figure reels danced invariably to the tune of *Miss McLeod* is an example.

The spectacular and difficult dances for the few were cultivated to the neglect of the simple ones for the many, leaving the social side untouched, except to criticise, or condemn. The ballroom dances in vogue at the time were the Quadrilles, or Sets, Lancers, Valse, Polka, Schottische or Barn Dance, Two Step, and Mazurka. These were all banned and nothing put in their place but a couple of long dances.

An exception should have been made, one would imagine, in favour of the popular old Sets (that had become Irishised), if only on account of the fine old tunes with which they were usually associated ; but they were decried amongst the rest.

It seems strange that such a policy should have been decided upon and pursued considering that no substitutes were provided beyond those mentioned. A few years later, however, the *Bridge of Athlone*, *Siege of Ennis*, and an incomplete form of *Haste to the Wedding* were introduced, but, as might have been expected, these simple contre dances proved inadequate as substitutes for all those that had been prohibited. The showy and intricate four and eight-hand jigs and reels of the Revival, although interesting to the spectator, were generally looked on as designed only for competition or display on account of their difficulty, and, consequently, had no appeal as social dances. A praiseworthy effort was made some years ago by Bean Sheain O Cuirrin of Limerick in arranging a new dance for couples on Irish lines suitable for the ballroom, but it has not, so far, appeared beyond a rather limited circle. It is to be regretted that this, and others of a similar nature had not been provided earlier, and popularised, as they would have removed the anomaly complained of as well as helping as a protection against those corrupt foreign influences that have been creeping in, and spreading so widely amongst us, for the past decade, or more.

B'fheidir na taithneoch gach a bfhuil scriobhte agam thuas le cach, ach ni mor an fhirinne a radh ma's mian linn an sceal do leigheas.

The object of this " Note " is not to apportion blame or affix censure, but to suggest that a united effort should now be made to remedy as far as possible the mistakes and errors of the past.

NOTE ON IRISH DANCING—*continued.*

The Double Jig appears to have been regarded by those not conversant with Irish dancing as the most admired and favoured of our national dances because of the much larger number of tunes in that classification, and of hearing them oftener apart from dancing than the others. The disparity in this respect between the jigs and the hornpipes, for example, indicates no preference whatever for this dance beyond the reel or the hornpipe by dancers, but it probably denotes a greater liking for its simpler rhythm by the average player, or the unskilled musician. This disproportion may be explained by stating that our old music abounded in airs and tunes of the jig type, and that very many of them have been utilised for the dance, or adapted to it, and classified as double jigs, while in the hornpipe, the tunes are for the greater part original. At present the Double is danced only as a bout consisting of elaborate and difficult steps, but, formerly, it also included a range of easy steps called the " Moinin Jig " which was in much request on social occasions.

The Reel, in the old style, had two distinct sets or ranges of steps—single and double. The former, being simple, were danced to lively tunes in single or two-four time, while for the latter, which are of a difficult hornpipe character, the slower old double reel tunes in ₵ time were employed. The steps, as a whole, ranged from very easy to very difficult. As a social dance with partners it was a general favourite, for many of the steps were so easy that young and old could participate. The double steps towards the end (if used) were danced by the girls with a becoming grace, and free from any appearance of vulgarity. When danced as a bout it comprised a selection from both ranges of steps. These formed a splendid item—varied, robust, and enthusing ; the music contributing in no small degree thereto, for two tunes contrasting in style were required for its performance. The change from one to the other was made on a signal from the dancers—usually a promenade in the bout, and hands across in the other case. In comparing the merits of this truly national and fine dance with the feeble, flurried, forced, and generally inferior style of that which has been put in its place the conclusion to be drawn is obvious.

The Single, or Ladies' Hornpipe, to which reference has already been made, was a special set of steps for the fair sex. They ranged from very easy to moderately difficult, and were in many respects not unlike the more advanced steps of the single reel, excluding their peculiar hornpipe finish. In style it was, appropriately, light, easy and graceful, and was danced to the lively simple tunes in two-four time. The Male, or Double Hornpipe, with which we are all familiar, is composed of difficult trebling steps, and necessitates the employment of the slower and more complex tunes in ₵ time for performance.

All noisy masculine movements of the drumming and grinding description were rigidly excluded from female dancing by the old masters, and both the shuffle and light batter used instead. The teachers of the old school were strict regarding style and neatness of execution, and were of courteous manner. They were carefully and thoroughly trained for their calling, and taught the art to their sons, so that the traditional style became a heritage which it was their privilege to preserve and to impart to others—a duty which they performed with the utmost fidelity. Alas, that this fine old type should have passed away, and that we should be compelled to witness so much that is spurious and vulgar, and altogether at variance with our great traditions.

The Single and Hop Jigs, although danced as bouts, are mainly social dances. They are of a simple, sprightly and graceful character and include steps and figures ; for example, the slip and side-steps for changing places, hands across and hands four round alternatively.

Regarding our national dances in general, it may be observed that the Slip or Hop Jig is the oldest as well as the most characteristic of them. Other nations also have their gigas, reels, and hornpipes, but none of them a dance in any respect like this. We can, therefore, claim it as being exclusively our own.

The Fling has been danced in Ireland for generations and is the only dance in which gestures are used. The steps are varied and interesting, some of the movements resembling those of the Single Jig.

Set Dances are special solo dances or " bouts " resembling the jig, reel and hornpipe in character, but, owing to their irregular structure in comparison with them, are more difficult, and demand a more finished technique from the performer. They have always appealed, accordingly, to accomplished dancers as a medium giving full scope for a display of skill and dexterity. We have about twenty of these fine dances, and in such a variety of style and rhythm as to embrace all our step dances, but, with the exception of the "Blackbird," and one or two others, they have been sadly neglected all these years during which we have been surfeited with "Miss McLeod" and her progeny. Apart from those in one movement only, their chief peculiarity lies in the irregularity of form or development of the second movement which constitutes the " Set." This varies from four to twelve bars in length and generally modulates into the first movement, or a strain thereof, with which it is brought to a close. Competitions were usually decided in former times, particularly between rival teachers, according to the degree of proficiency displaced by the competitors—often on a soaped table—in all these dances.

NOTE ON IRISH DANCING—*continued.*

Rinnci Fada are simple social dances in which any number of couples may take part. There are about ten of these Long or Contre Dances, five of which call for no special reference, or comment, as they are regularly danced at Ceilidhthe, and sometimes at other reunions also. Details regarding An Rinnce Mor, and the Fairy Reel would be of little use here, for they are more elaborate than the others, and an adequate knowledge of them can only be acquired where they are taught, or practiced. The Cotillion was formerly well known in the south, but it is now, apparently, quite forgotten ; the tune is inserted in this volume not so much in the expectation of its revival as in the hope that a new dance may be supplied to replace it. The " Limerick Lasses " is a quiet easy dance in quadrille, or reel time. The dancers stand in two lines opposite their partners—gents with left shoulders to top. First couple join hands and lead down the middle, and return (8 bars) ; change sides, balence, or set to 2nd lady and gent respectively and turn (8 bars) ; face partners, set and turn (8 bars) ; lead down, and return as before ; change sides, and dance with 3rd lady and gent. When the 3rd couple has been danced with, the 2nd joins in after the 1st and so on until all are engaged. When the leading couples reach the end, having danced with all in succession, they fall back to their respective sides, remain in line and keep moving gradually up until reaching their original position. To finish, advance, retire and turn partners. Should a very large number be engaged, and the dance considered too long, it may be brought to a close whenever desired, or by the dancers falling out as they reach the end until only two couples remain, who may wind up by dancing some reel steps. " Haste to the Wedding " is a lively dance in jig time. The dancers range themselves in two lines as in the " Limerick Lasess." First couple step forward to about a pace from each other before commencing. Change places, balence twice (heel, toe and grind for gents), and turn partner (8 bars) ; lead down and return (8 bars) ; hands three around with 2nd lady, gallopade by left (4 bars), form an arch allowing her to pass through during accented notes, and change hands (4 bars) ; repeat figure with 2nd gent, and resume starting position (8 bars) ; next time hands round with 3rd couple, after which 2nd couple join in, and so on to the end. This dance may be concluded in a similar manner to the previous one, the steps, of course, in this case being of the jig variety. Sir Roger, though not of Irish origin, has, like the Fling, been danced here for generations. It is a simple lively dance in 9/8 or slip time, and is uncommon on that account. A description of it may be found in a Ballroom Guide.

Hop Jig tunes lend themselves admirably to contre dances like Sir Roger, as the Double Jig tunes do to the " Kerry Dance," " Haste to the Wedding," etc., while the Single Time has always been a great favourite for some figures of the old sets.

The habit of dancing too fast and accelerating the speed, so prevalent of late years, should be checked and discouraged ; it tends to spoil the effect of both dance and tune and is at variance with the traditional style in which the pace was moderate and steady. This undesirable practice is particularly noticeable in the Single Reel, which is usually danced nowadays ar nós an sidhe gaoithe.

Children's deportment should be attended to during the course of their training so that they may not dance with their toes turned in, or with shoulders stooped or contracted.

Irish Dancing is cultural, graceful and diversified, it is also manly and athletic, and, as stated on high authority, " it *does not* make degenerates." The difficulty of step dancing has often been made to serve as an excuse for the apathy and indifference of many towards Irish Dancing altogether, but we have a number of interesting figure and other dances, some so simple that all may take part in them.

Pernicious and degrading foreign influences must be combated and suppressed if our dancing and music are to be restored to their rightful place in the social life of our people.

P. de R.

Nodlag, 1927.

THE ROCHE COLLECTION OF TRADITIONAL IRISH MUSIC

COLLECTION OF IRISH AIRS

Volume III.

INDEX

AIRS

SLIGO AIR

DEATH AND THE SINNER

eaṁonn a' chnuic — nós na ronne

Bruacha na Bearbha
THE BANKS OF THE BARROW
Andante con espress
4
LIMERICK TOWN
from HUGHES
Moderately slow
5
THE POITIN STILL
Spirited
6

THE BONNIE GREEN TREE
Allegretto
7
ULSTER AIR
Andante
8
MY LAGAN LOVE
from HUGHES
Rather slow
9
mo craoibhin aoibhin aulinn ó
Plaintively
10
p
mf
p

BANDON BRIDGE
Andante con moto
11
Barr an Chnuic
THE HILL TOP
Allegretto con grazia
12
Gleanntán-Araglin Aoibinn
BEAUTIFUL ARAGLIN
Gracefully
13
OH PLEASANT WERE THE DAYS
Graceful and plaintive
14
WHERE THE AUGBEG FLOWS
Moderato
15

Maiġreaḋ Ḋílis Ḃreaṫnaċ

Uair roiṁ ḃreacaḋ an lae *or* FAREWELL TO ARDMALE

Staic an ṁargaiḋ

Sroṫán na mangaire bréige or YOU'LL NEVER DECEIVE ME AGAIN
Moderato
19
Ca rabais anois a cailín ḃig
Andante
20
Tá mo ġráḋ geal dom ṫréigint MY FAIR LOVE IS LEAVING ME
With feeling
21
Mo ġraḋ é an cruisgín agus é lán THE OLD JUG AND IT FULL
Rather slow
22
1
3

*1st Setting Nº 48. Vol 1.

IT'S DOWN IN YON VALLEY WHERE VIOLETS GREW
Gracefully
26
p
mf
p
SLIAB FÉIDLIM
Rather slow, with feeling
27
SUANTRAI CIARRAIGHE
Slow
28
THE PEARL OF THE IRISH NATION
Moderato molto
29

An Cailín Deas Donn
THE PRETTY BROWN GIRL
Andante con espress.
30
Ceann Deiġinse
THE MEETING OF THE WATERS
Moderato elegante
31
mf
cresc.
p
rit.
mf
17
cresc.
f
5
tr
Cadenza
rit.
Tá mo ġráḋ ġeal imṫiġṫe or THE GALLANT WHITE HORSEMAN
Plaintively
32

An Clár Bog Déil
Maestoso appassionata
33
THE WANDERER'S MUSINGS, or THE WORKS OF THE LAND
Gracefully
34
1.
Last
D.C.
THE GENTLE MAIDEN, or MEN OF THE WEST
Andante con moto
35
KELLY THE BOY FROM KILANE
Maestoso marziale
36
1.
2.

An Laoċra·
F. R.
Allegretto con grazia
37
p
mf
Fáinne geal an lae
Moderato
38
BELIEVE ME IF ALL, from MOORE
Andante con espress.
39
Sláinte na nGaodhal
Moderato
40

CARRAIG DONN

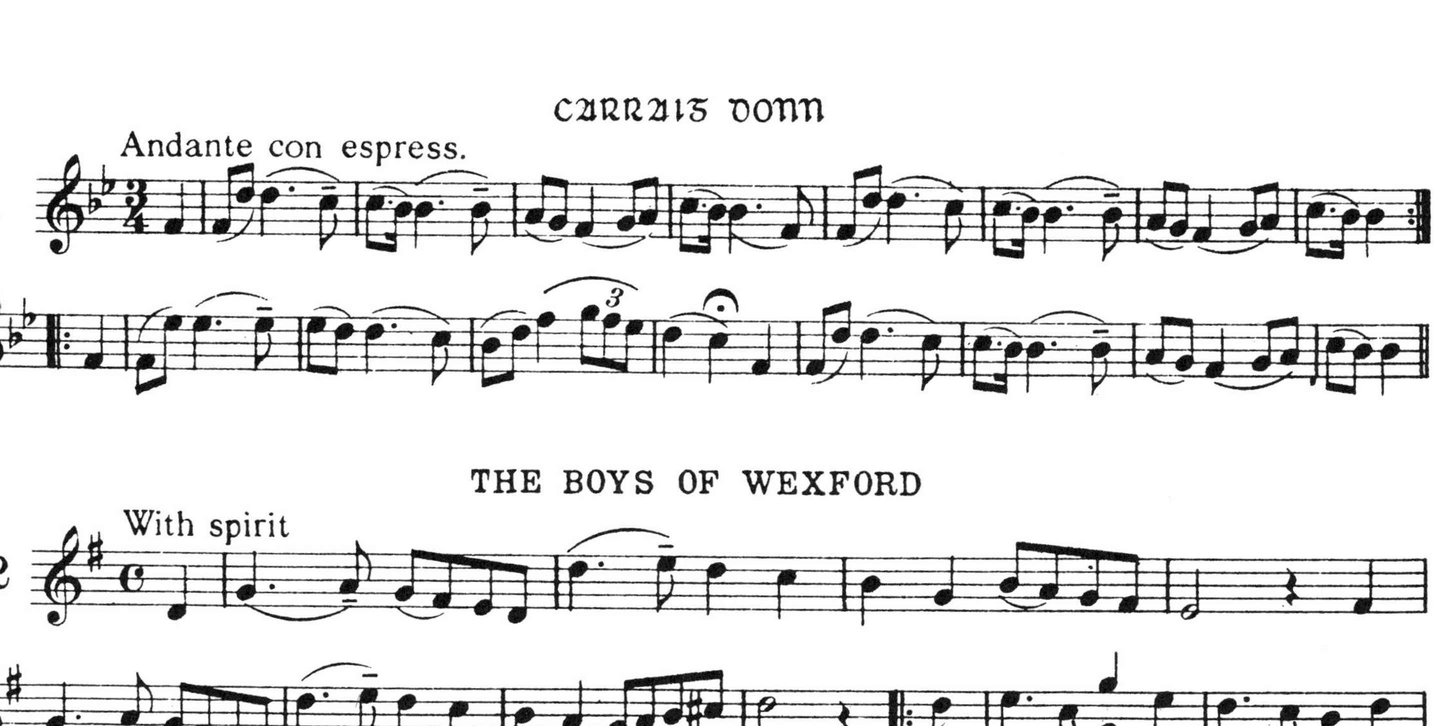

CAILÍN DEAS CRÚIḊTE NA MBÓ

HAS SORROW THY YOUNG DAYS SHADED

THE FOGGY DEW
Moderato
45
VIVE LA!
With spirit
46
FANAID GROVE
Dolce
47
BILLY BYRNE OF BALLYMANUS
Allegretto
48

EOCHAILL
Andante
49
THE MAIDS OF MOURNE SHORE
Plaintively
50
FAREWELL TO BALLINDERRY
Moderato semplice
51
KEVIN BARRY
Andante affetuoso
52

mo ġráḋ ġeal ḋílis
Rather slow and with feeling
53
p
mf
Cad.
mf
mp
rit.
SLIABH NA MBAN
Andantino
54
p
mf
p
1
2
Poco più mosso
an ḟáinleóġ ḃeag
Andante con espress.
55
1
2
Cronán
tr

I SAW THY FORM, from MOORE
Andante amoroso
56
SLIABH GALLEN
Andante maestoso con espress.
57
tr
O NATIVE MUSIC
Lover
Dolce e moderato molto
58
3
rit.

LAMENT FOR FATHER MICHAEL MOLONEY
(ORIGINAL AIR)

Jn. Roche

BINN LISHIN AERACH A' BHROGHA*
2nd SETTING

*(1st Setting page 19 Vol. 1)

Aer na Máidne

THE ENCHANTED VALLEY

Intro
CONTENTED I AM or THE BATTLE EVE
(with Variations)
F. R.
Allegro
68
Theme
Con spirito
Var. 1
Var. 2
Moderato

Var. 3
Var. 4
An Druimḟionn Donn Dílis
Andantino con espress.
69
Ullaċán Dubh O'
Rather slow and plaintive
70

REELS*

THE COTTAGE IN THE GROVE

71

LORD ST. CLAIR'S REEL

72

THE FLYING COLUMN

73

*See prefatory note

THE WAYSIDE WAGGON
74
CUMAR NA CATHRACH
75
O FLAHERTY'S GAMBLE
76
TRIPPING THRO' THE MEADOWS
77

AN COLAMÓIR SÚGAĊ
78
5
BUMPER ALLEN'S DELIGHT
79
1
2
THE TEETOTALLERS
2nd SETTING
80
3
4

THE EIGHT AND FORTY SISTERS

THE GALTY RANGERS
84
TOUCH ME IF YOU DARE
85
ᵹleann coise binne
2nd SETTING
86
THE CROOKED WAY TO DUBLIN
2nd SETTING
87

DOUBLE JIGS*

THE PRIEST'S LEAP

* See note

THE CATHOLIC BOY

Tart ar an Ól
94
Hurry the Jug
95
Baois na n-Óige
The Follies of Youth
96

Geátsai na Leibide
THE AWKWARD CLOWN'S ANTICS
97
An Cailín ab Ḟearr Liom
THE GIRL FOR ME
98
Uġdarás gan Eolas
99

FAREWELL TO LIBERTY

Ailteóiri na Cille *or* THE GALBALLY FARMER

THE RAKES OF KILDARE

SINGLE JIGS

NA MADRAÍ 'SAN EÓRNA

BRUISE THE PEASE

108

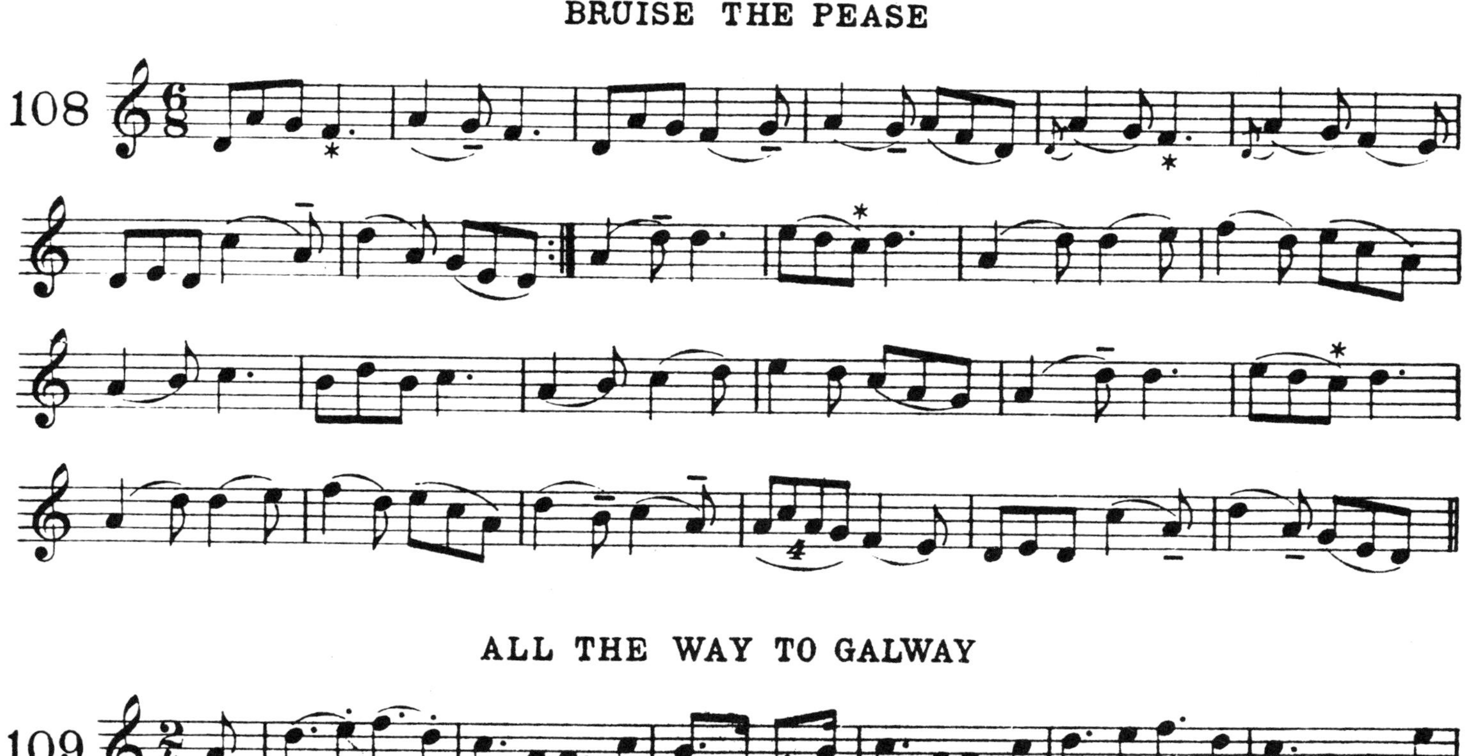

ALL THE WAY TO GALWAY

109

GIOLLA NA GRUAIGE BÁINE THE FAIR HAIRED LAD

110

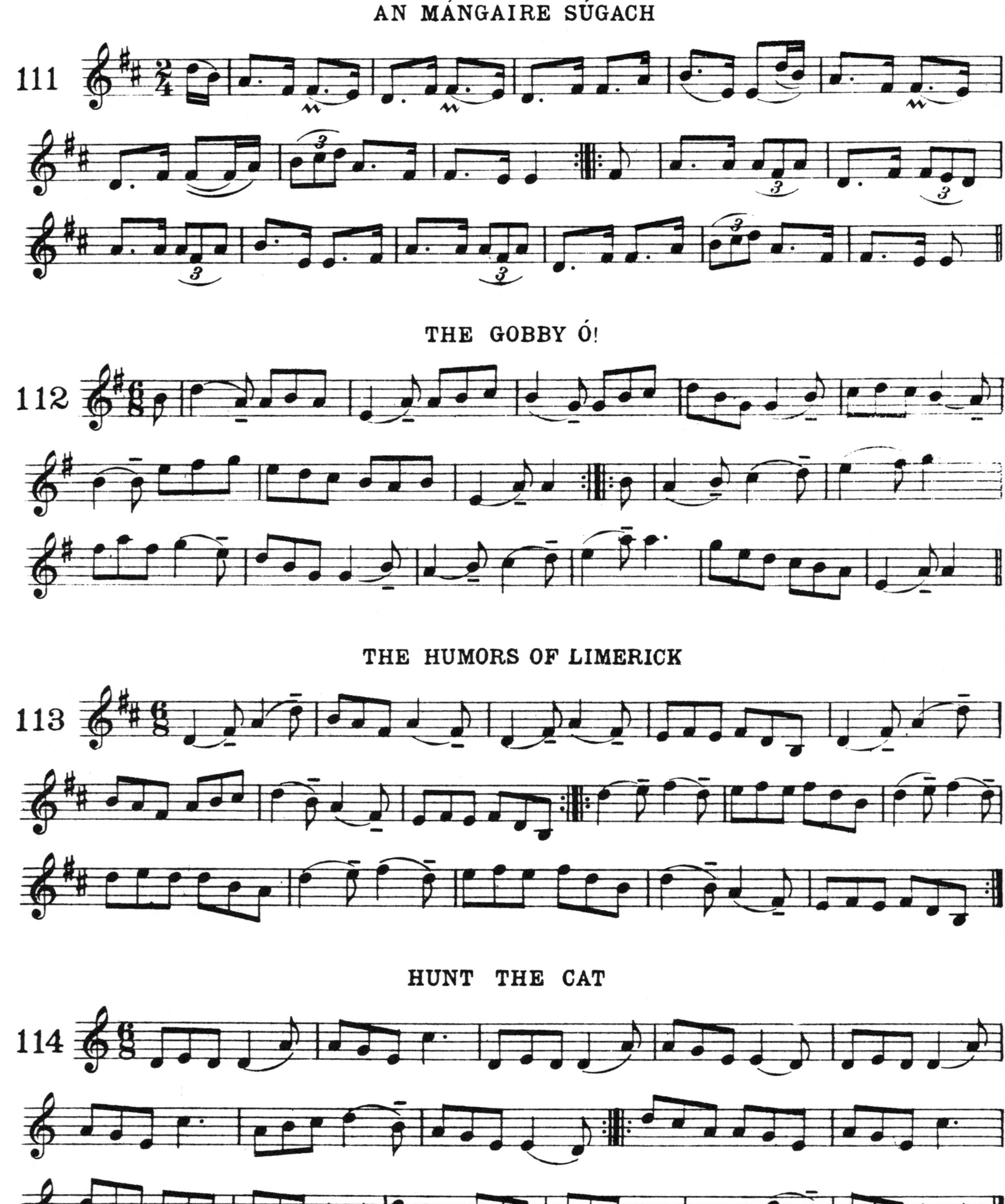
AN MÁNGAIRE SÚGACH
111
THE GOBBY Ó!
112
THE HUMORS OF LIMERICK
113
HUNT THE CAT
114

HOP JIGS

THE HILLS OF TIPPERARY
115
1
2
Lá na Féile
HOP JIG OR COUNTRY DANCE
116
THE BUCKSKIN BREECHES
117
Ceol na Seilge
THE SPORT OF THE CHASE
118

OLD SET TUNES

122

123

124

125

126
1
2
127
128
129

130

131

132

133

134

LONG DANCES*

An Rinnce Mór

*See note

THE WAVES OF TOREY

136

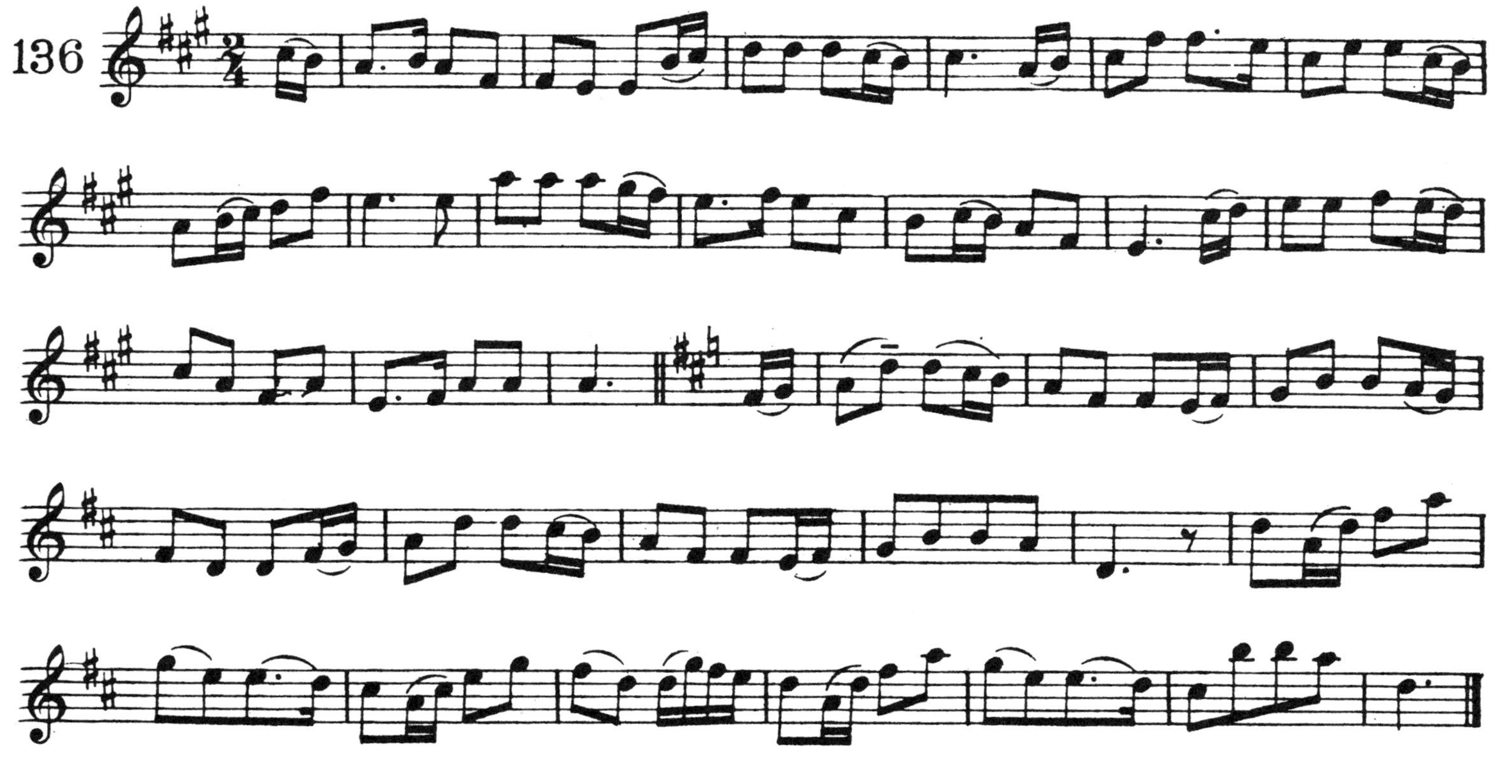

THE WALLS OF LIMERICK

137

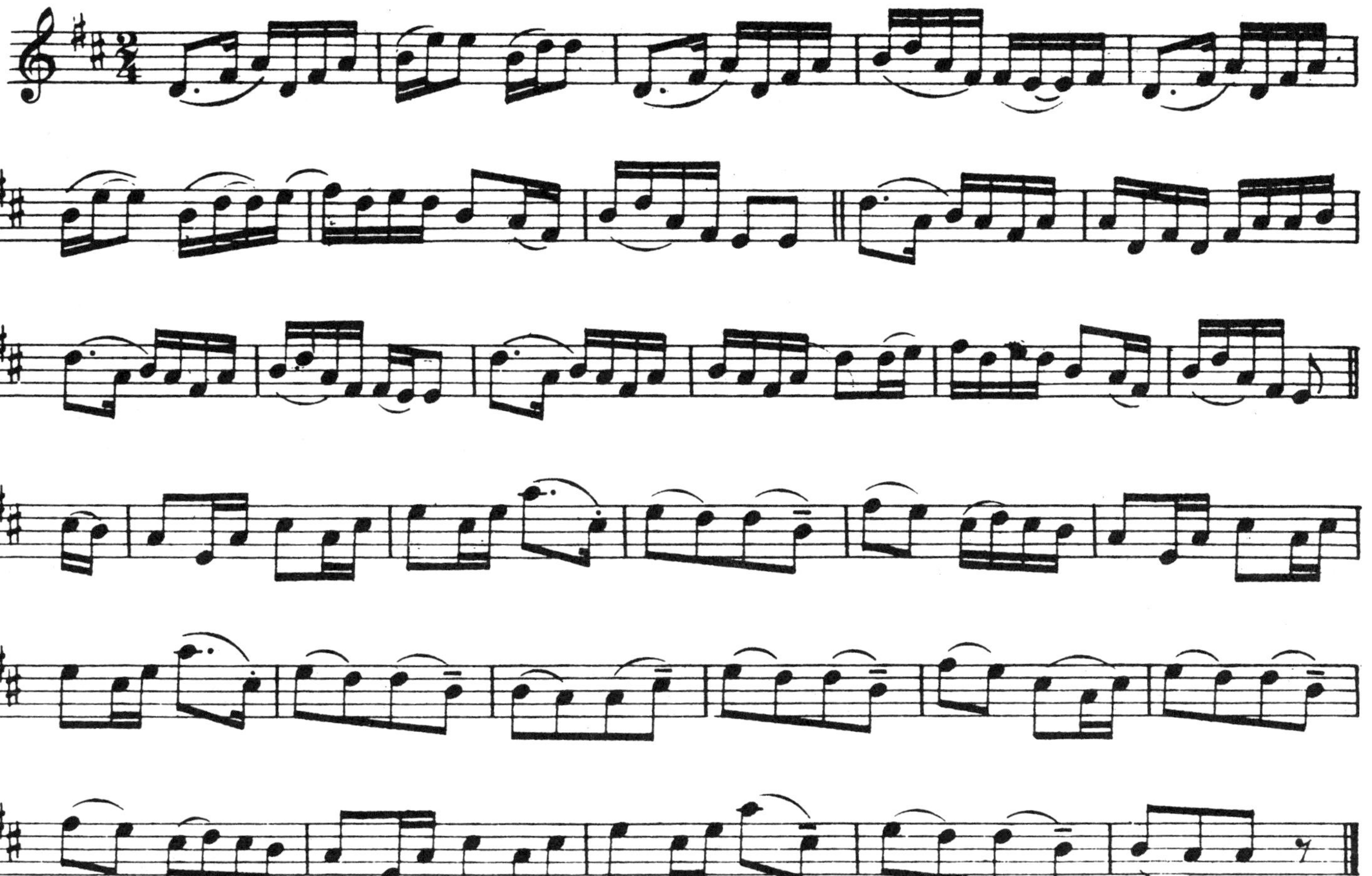

RINNCE NA SIDEÓGA
THE FAIRY DANCE
138
1.
2.
Last
D.C.
1.
2.
Last time go from 𝄐 to ⊕ D.C.
SUIDE NA h-INSE
THE SIEGE OF ENNIS
139
1.
2.
Repeat 8va
1.
2.
Repeat 8va adlib.

Droiċead Aṫa Luain
THE BRIDGE OF ATHLONE
140
THE COTILLION
141

OLD DANCES (not Irish by origin)

THE DEW-DROP WALTZ

142

SUMMER FLOWER
SCHOTTISCHE

143

D. C.
Trio
D. C.
THE ROSE WALTZ
144
1
D.C.
2
D.C.

CASTLES IN THE AIR
SCHOTTISCHE
145
THE BUTTERFLY
POLKA
146
D. C.
Trio
D. C.
NYMPH OF THE WAVE
WALTZ
147
1
Repeat 8va

2
HAZEL DELL
SCHOTTISCHE
148
1
2nd time 8va
2
D. C.
Trio
D. C.

MARTHA
VALSE

149

THE LIMERICK WALTZ
OR REDOWA

151

Trio

"THE BARNACLE" REDOWA

152

PULL DOWN THE BLIND
WALTZ

153

1

2

FORGET ME NOT

POLKA

154

THE FAIRY SPELL

WALTZ

155

OLD TIMES
SCHOTTISCHE

156

THAT OLD VIOLIN TUNE
WALTZ

BIDDY BARRY
SCHOTTISCHE

THE DARKIES' DREAM
BARN-DANCE

MEDLEY TWO-STEP

THE RAZZLE DAZZLE
BARN DANCE

HUMMING BIRD
WALTZ
163
1.
2.
Rep! 8va
D.C.
"NAPPER TANDY"
REDOWA, OR MAZURKA
Allegretto
164
3
1.
2.
Waltz time
1.
Last
D.C.

AILEEN ALANNA
WALTZ

165

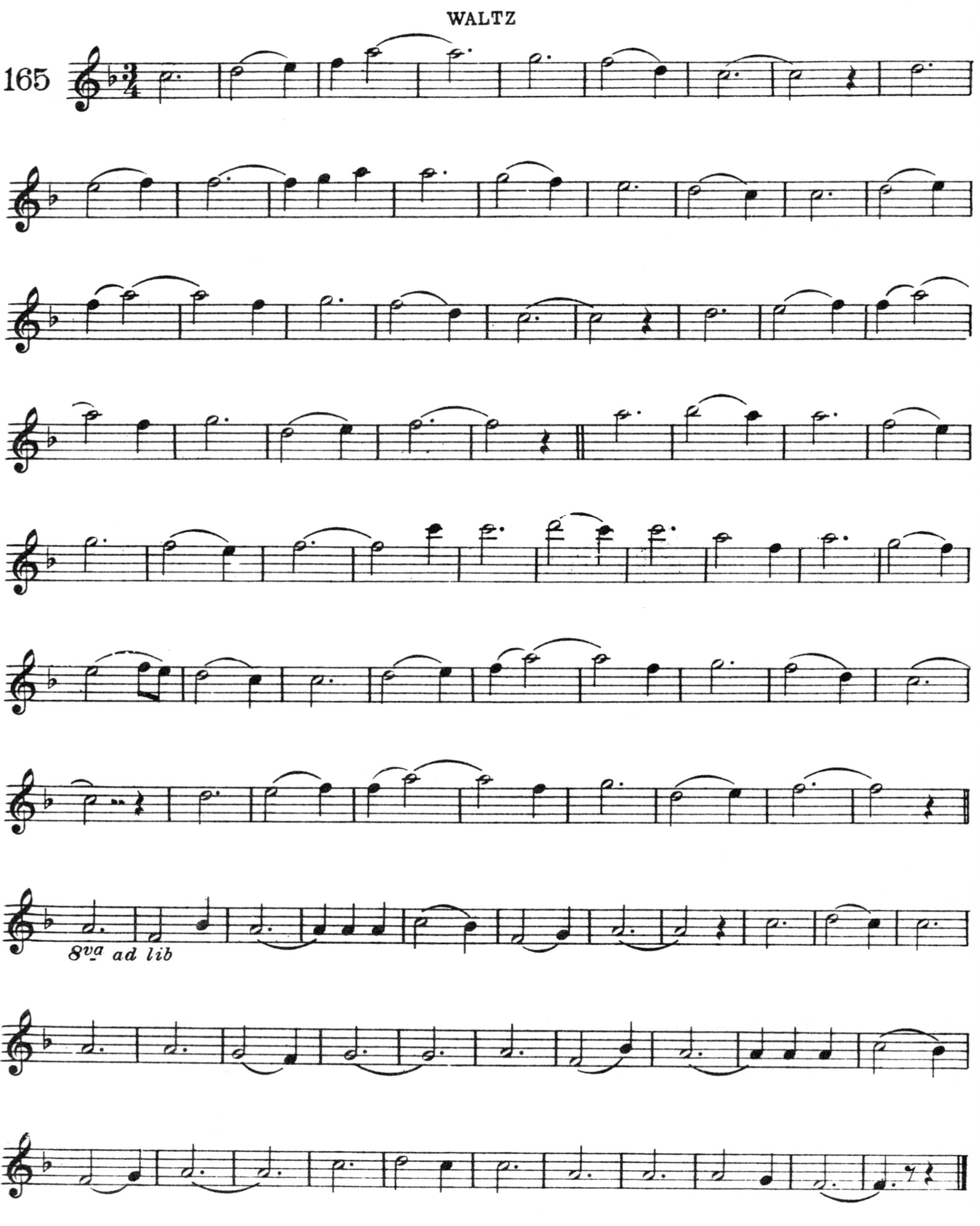

KATE KEARNEY
WALTZ

166

HORNPIPES*

DUNPHY'S

167

THE TRESHERS

168

SARATOGA HORNPIPE

169

* See prefatory note

AN SPEALADOIR *or* THE CUCKOO'S NEST
(2nd SETTING)

170

THE LODGE GATE

171

THE THIEVING MAGPIE

172

+Left hand piz

Ingar do Ṡuiḋe Finn

MORDUANT'S HORNPIPE

Fáilte go h-Éirinn

FRAOĊ NA N-AÉ *or* BRIAN THE BRAVE

179

THE BOYS OF BALLYCAHILL

180

WIGS ON THE GREEN

181

Ciuṁais na móna or PRETTY MAGGIE MORRISSEY
182
1.
2.
THE BOYS OF BLUEHILL
183
DANCING ON THE GREEN
184
1.
2.
1.
2.

SET DANCES*

THE ACE AND DEUCE OF PIPERING

YOUGHAL HARBOUR

BONAPARTE'S RETREAT
(2nd SETTING)

*See note

An Rácaire Fánaċ THE RAMBLING RAKE
from O'NEILL. with corrections
188

THE THREE CAPTAINS

from **O'NEILL**. *slightly altered*

THE LODGE ROAD

from O'NEILL *slightly altered*

THE DRUNKEN GAUGER

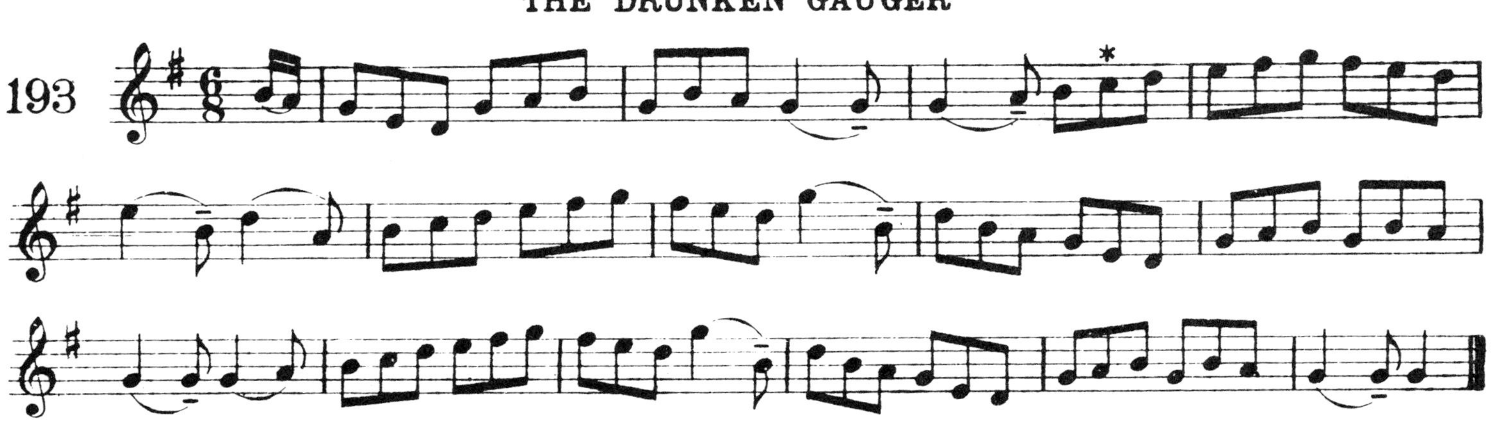

QUADRILLES

na seana laeṫeannta sona THOSE HAPPY DAYS

4

5

Ʒıo' sean nı. críon OLD YET NEW QUADRILLE

195

4
1st & 3rd
D.C.
2nd & 4th
D.C.
5
mf
ff
1st & 3rd
D.C.
2nd & 4th
1
2
D.C.

NA h-OÍÓCEANNEA SUILCNIAŢRE — NIGHTS OF GLADNESS QUADRILLE

4

5

THE ARRAVALE ROVERS

QUADRILLE

4
1st & 3rd
D. C.
2nd & 4th
8va
ad lib.
D. C.
5
p
f
1st & 3rd
D. C.
2nd & 4th
8va ad lib.
D. C.

MARCHES

MOUNTCASHEL'S BRIGADE

O'BRIEN OF ARRA

TRIUMPHAL MARCH
205
Repeat 8va ad lib
An ċeolsiḋe fánsé
THE WANDERING MINSTREL
Moderato
206
OLD ROLLING CORK
Lively
207

CAPTAIN DUNNE'S MARCH
208
MAIRSEÁIL NA N-ÓGLAĊ
MARCH OF THE VOLUNTEERS
209
MO ĊEOIL SIḂ A LAOĊRA
Moderato
210
THE MAIDS OF ARAGLEN
Moderato
211

THE PLEASURES OF HOPE
Cheerfully
212
Toichim na Sean-Shaodhal
213
DOWN AT THE SEASIDE
Moderato
214
TURKEYS IN THE STRAW
Allegretto
215

FINGAL MARCH
Go dána
216
Aṁrán na n-Óglaċ
Tempo di marcia
217
1
Last

airs

double jigs

single jigs

hop jigs

set dances

flings

old set dances

long dances

quadrilles

marches etc.

reels

hornpipes

old dances